DOLPHIN ISLAND

Storm Clouds

Read all the books in the *Dolphin Island* series:

Jenny Oldfield

DOLPHIN ISLAND

Storm Clouds

Illustrations by
Daniel Howarth

Hodder
Children's
Books

For lovely Lola, Jude and Evan – three dedicated dolphin fans

HODDER CHILDREN'S BOOKS

First published in Great Britain in 2018 by Hodder and Stoughton

1 3 5 7 9 10 8 6 4 2

Text copyright © Jenny Oldfield, 2018

Inside illustrations copyright © Daniel Howarth, 2018

The moral rights of the author and illustrator have been asserted.

A CIP catalogue record for this book is available from the British Library.

ISBN 978 1 444 92832 7

Typeset in ITC Caslon 224

Printed and bound in Great Britain by Clays Ltd, Elcograf S.p.A.

The paper and board used in this book are made from wood
from responsible sources.

Hodder Children's Books
An imprint of Hachette Children's Group
Part of Hodder and Stoughton
Carmelite House
50 Victoria Embankment
London EC4Y 0DZ

An Hachette UK Company
www.hachette.co.uk

www.hachettechildrens.co.uk

Chapter One

'Boo!' Mia Fisher crept up on her older brother, Alfie, while he was sleeping under a palm tree.

He awoke with a sudden jerk then sprang to his feet. 'That's not funny!' he yelled after her as she sprinted down the beach.

'Can't catch me!' she cried over her shoulder.

'Seriously, Mia – don't.' Alfie was unhappy as he brushed sand from his red shorts and jammed his straw hat more firmly on his head. 'You're always doing stuff like that; making me jump and scaring me to death.'

His thirteen-year-old sister, Fleur, slowly opened one eye and then the other. 'She's seven. Annoying people is what seven-year-olds do.' Once she was sure that Mia had stopped at the water's edge, she closed her eyes and carried on with her siesta.

'She'd better not do it again.' Eleven-year-old Alfie went on grumbling as he left the shade of the palm tree and walked towards the family shelter built out of bamboo canes and palm leaves. The sturdy structure was raised on stilts and had a platform made from salvaged wooden planks thrown up on to the beaches of Dolphin Island at high tide. The thatched roof was secured with old rope and lianas from the tropical jungle that covered the high mountain peak at the centre of the island. The Fishers had built their home strongly to stand up to hurricane force winds that swept in off the blue ocean, often hitting without warning and tearing up most things that lay in their path. Alfie climbed on to the platform and watched through narrowed eyes as Mia cavorted along the shoreline.

She laughed as a wave broke against nearby rocks and she felt the cool spray shower down over her head. She danced through the foam that swirled around her ankles then she cartwheeled back up the beach towards him. 'Play I-spy!' she clamoured. 'I spy with my little eye something beginning with ...'

'No way,' Alfie mumbled, disappearing inside the shelter as she drew near.

'It's OK, Mia – I'll play.' Fleur sat up with a sigh. She wiggled her toes in the warm white sand and glanced out to sea to check for dolphins. The calm blue water sparkled on without interruption, out past the reef where their yacht, *Merlin*, had sunk and onwards to the dazzling, flat horizon.

'Yay! … Something beginning with M!'

'Mountain?'

'Nope.'

'Millipede?' Fleur pointed to a reddish-brown specimen with black spots undulating up a nearby tree trunk. She calculated that it was at least twenty centimetres long.

'No.'

'Mum?'

'No. Anyway, you can't see her. She's at Lookout Point with Dad.'

Fair enough. 'OK, I give in.'

'Monkey!' Mia lifted her hat to reveal her furry friend. She tossed him high in the air and attempted

3

to catch him but he landed in the sand at Fleur's feet.

'Poor Monkey.' Fleur picked him up and dusted him down. The battered soft toy, a survivor of shipwreck, storm and fire, had only one eye and a bald patch on top of his head. Fleur held him to her chest and pretended to cuddle him.

Suddenly serious, Mia knelt down beside her. After more than seven weeks on the island, her brown hair had turned blonde at the tips and her hazel eyes shone brightly in her round, tanned face. Around her neck she wore a mother-of-pearl charm in the shape of a dolphin and she had a string of shells around her waist over a turquoise swimsuit that had faded to pale blue. 'I've got a cool idea,' she said to Fleur. 'We could make an eyepatch for Monkey.'

'I guess we could,' Fleur's answer was cautious and the corners of her mouth twitched as she tried not to smile. 'It might make him look like a pirate though.'

'Hmm.' Mia tilted her head to one side to consider this. 'Yay, a pirate!' She snatched the toy monkey from Fleur then sprinted towards the shelter. 'Alfie, guess what – we're going to make an eyepatch for Monkey.

4

He'll be a pirate!'

Animal-mad Fleur let the smile appear. *Cute*, she thought as she rested back on her elbows. *But give me a real live monkey any day.*

She lay back in the sand and stared up at the palm leaf canopy. Seven weeks on Dolphin Island felt like a whole lifetime. It seemed an age since *Merlin* had been caught in a storm in the Torres Strait and had capsized in the mountainous waves. Fleur relived the fear that she'd felt when she, Alfie and Mia had scrambled up on deck just in time, only to be tossed overboard without knowing what had happened to Katie and James, their mum and dad, or whether the current would sweep them to dry land or further out to sea. And then the magical moment when their dolphins had appeared out of nowhere; three grey, domed heads emerging from the waves, whistling and clicking above the roaring wind, as if each one was saying, *Grab my fin. Hold on tight!* She remembered the miracle that was Pearl, Jazz and Stormy carrying them all safely to the shore.

Fleur took a deep breath then let out a loud sigh.

The Fisher family had come through so much since then. They'd landed on the uninhabited island and found shelter in George's Cave. The storm had passed and the next day Mum and Dad had found them and there'd been a happy reunion. They'd all pulled together to build a rough shelter and find fresh water at Butterfly Falls. They'd lit a fire and learned how to fish with the help of their faithful dolphin friends when Jazz, Stormy and Pearl had swum into the bay and driven shoals of silver fish into Fleur and Alfie's primitive net.

And that had only been the beginning. Ships, boats and planes had passed without noticing the smoke from their fires or their pleas for help written in giant letters in the wet sand. Hopes of rescue had risen then faded like the trail of vapour left behind by the planes. There'd been more storms, plus a fire started by marauding macaque monkeys that had destroyed their first shelter and all their belongings, then finally a shark attack that had left Alfie's precious Pearl fighting for survival. *So much!* Fleur thought with a sigh.

The life that she'd lived before Dolphin Island now

seemed unreal. Once upon a time she'd gone to school and hung out with friends. She'd washed her hair whenever she'd wanted, followed fashions and watched YouTube videos. She'd seen capuchin monkeys and tree kangaroos on wildlife documentaries but never until now in real life.

It was the same for Alfie. He'd been a maths geek and techie, and he'd known everything about the navigation system aboard *Merlin*. Now he used a stick of charcoal to draw a map of Dolphin Island on sailcloth and carved notches on to a calendar stick to mark off the days.

Thursday. Day 53. It felt like for ever.

'Fleur, look at this!' Mia jumped down from the platform and ran towards her, holding Monkey aloft. 'Alfie did it. He made him an eyepatch out of a blue plastic bottle top and a piece of string he found on Turtle Beach. It's so cool! Look!'

*

After siesta came afternoon chores.

'Let's all do water,' Fleur suggested when she and Mia joined Alfie under the shelter awning. 'After that we can split up. I volunteer to keep the fire going here at base camp.'

'And I'll beachcomb for firewood in Black Crab Cove.' Alfie jumped in quickly with his own decision.

'Cool.' The plan was agreed and Fleur handed out the plastic containers they would use to collect water from the falls. They were in no hurry as they scaled the narrow cliff path in single file, stopping to check out a small group of macaque monkeys perched on a ledge above their heads. One of the youngsters picked up a nearby stone and tossed it towards them.

'Missed!' Mia said with a laugh as the stone rattled past them on to the beach below.

'That's not very nice,' Alfie muttered as the monkey family scampered off.

Fleur took in every detail. She watched them whisk their long tails and run on all fours, turning their tufted heads and chattering excitedly at the human intruders.

'Water!' Alfie reminded her from behind.

Butterfly Falls lay a hundred metres ahead. They could hear the fresh water splashing on to rocks and saw a cloud of white butterflies rise from myrtle

shrubs overhanging the falls. The way was fringed by tall grasses and flowers of every colour, providing good camouflage for green cane toads, tree frogs, chameleons and other small lizards.

'Wow!' Fleur said as she came across a colony of pale grey bats clinging to crevices in the dark red cliff face. She took a closer look and recognized the tiny creatures' big ears, thin wings and leathery skin. 'They're lesser mouse-tails.'

'Yuck!' Mia made a face and squeezed past with her empty container.

Alfie stayed behind to scan the sea spread out below them. He was looking for dolphins, of course.

'Anything?' Fleur asked when at last she tore herself away from the fascinating bats.

'Nope.' The bay was empty. 'Zilch.'

'Maybe later.' Like Alfie, Fleur longed for Jazz, Stormy and Pearl to put in an appearance. 'Don't worry – Pearl will be OK now that she's rejoined her pod.'

'I know she will,' he said slowly. But the reunion had only happened yesterday. Before that he'd had to nurse his dolphin friend back to health after the tiger shark's attack. It had been touch and go at first; the jagged wound had been deep and Pearl had been separated from her pod, hidden in the swamp off Mangrove Bay, unable to fish or fend for herself. 'I can't help wondering how she is though.'

'I get it.' Fleur gave him a reassuring smile. 'But the sun's shining, the sky's blue. We have to chill and enjoy this peace and quiet while we can.'

Together they followed Mia up the path and joined her by the waterfall where she sat on a rock dangling her feet in the cool water, wearing a smile from ear to ear. 'I spy with my little eye ...' she began.

'Not now, Mi-mi.' Alfie squatted down to fill his container.

'Something beginning with D!' She pointed out to sea. 'D – D – Dol ...'

Alfie jumped up and scanned the horizon. 'Where?'

'There, in the bay – dolphins!'

Fleur shaded her eyes with her hand. Mia was right – a pod of twenty or so were swimming into view from behind the reef. Some breached the water and soared through the clear air while others rode the foaming crest of the waves. Two at the rear of the pod slapped their tail flukes against the surface, splashing madly. One youngster turned on his back to show his pale belly and scud with his flippers in a lazy backstroke until his impatient mother did a U-turn and slapped him with her tail to hurry him along.

'I can see Stormy, there at the front!' Mia picked out her dark grey dolphin as he rose from the water, twisted in the air then re-entered with scarcely a splash.

'And Jazz.' Fleur laughed as her amazing acrobat friend raised his torpedo-shaped body out of the water and tail-walked across the bay. 'It's like he's doing his funny dance – look!'

But where was Pearl? Alfie's heart was in his mouth as he sorted the adults from the youngsters. He spotted a calf with a chubby body – so not that one – and another who was the right slim shape but who didn't display Pearl's pale pink underside as she leaped clear of the water – not that one either. Still he sought her out.

'Over there!' Fleur spotted Pearl before Alfie did.

She pointed to a young dolphin bringing up the rear.

And yes, there she was; dark grey on top with a pinkish-cream belly and a dorsal fin that was more curved than most, happily lob-tailing and creating a big splash as she swam along. Alfie laughed and raised his fist in triumph. 'Yeah!' Beautiful, amazing Pearl was fully recovered and able to keep up with her pod!

'Let's go and swim with them.' Mia was all for dropping her canister and racing back down the cliff path.

Fleur shook her head then looked at Alfie. 'We can't. Can we?'

'No. We've got jobs to do.'

'Plee-eease!' Mia pressed the palms of her hands together. 'Pretty please!'

'We can't,' Fleur insisted as she watched the wonderful dolphin display below. 'Anyway, the pod will be long gone by the time we get down to the beach.'

Alfie nodded his agreement. The dolphins had no intention of stopping in Base Camp Bay. They were heading for Turtle Beach, obviously on a mission to catch silversides and parrotfish, anchovies and snappers. But he'd caught sight of Pearl and laid his worries to rest. 'OK, Mi-mi, give me your favourite dolphin fact while we fill our bottles.'

Mia concentrated by screwing her mouth tight and wrinkling her nose. 'They can talk,' she finally announced.

'Kind of,' Alfie said as he dipped his container into the stream.

'Fleur said they could,' Mia reminded him. 'They chirp and click and whistle. That's proper dolphin language.'

'Dolphinnish.' Alfie grinned. He felt his anxious heart ease as he held his canister under the waterfall. 'How about you, Fleury?'

'I don't have one favourite fact. I love every single thing about them.' *Their sleek shape, the way the water runs off their shiny, velvety backs, their dark eyes that seem to know everything, their curved dorsal fins, the way they blow air out of the nostril on the top of their heads.* She could go on and on. 'Did you know – their brains are the same size as a human's?'

'That's what I like best,' Alfie chipped in. He straightened up to see that the dolphins had already left the bay. 'They're as clever as us.'

'Cleverer,' Fleur said quickly. 'They can use echolocation – we can't. They cruise underwater at speeds of up to thirty kilometres per hour. That's way faster than us. They …'

'OK, you win.' He was happy to concede the point. 'But even better than that, they bring good luck.' After fifty-three days on Dolphin Island Alfie was a firm believer. 'Look at what Pearl, Stormy and Jazz have done for us if you want proof.'

Mia looked thoughtful then held up the charm around her neck. 'Does that mean we can stop building our raft because the dolphins will send someone to rescue us from the island?'

Alfie glanced at Fleur then frowned. 'I don't know about that, Mi-mi.'

'But they bring good luck – you just said.'

Fleur sighed and looked down into the empty bay. She didn't want to dim her young sister's shiny dream. 'Maybe, one day,' she murmured.

'If I keep on wearing my lucky charm?'

'Yes, you do that.' Fleur gave Alfie a significant look

then sighed again. *It's better for Mia to go on hoping than to give up, isn't it?*

Alfie read Fleur's thoughts and turned away. *Maybe, maybe not.* 'Let's go, Mi-mi,' he said gruffly. 'After we've taken the water back to camp, you can come beachcombing with me.'

Chapter Two

The day's chores were done and Mia, Fleur and Alfie sat by the campfire with their dad and mum. Orange flames flickered and rose into the dusk sky, attracting big brown moths with grey furry bodies that flitted in circles above their heads. Parrots and cockatoos squawked from the palm trees as they settled down to roost, while two young monkeys perched on a rock close to the family's food store, daring each other to creep nearer still.

'Who would like more pudding?' James held out a clam shell plate with leftover strips of dried jackfruit.

Fleur and Alfie took one piece each, leaving two on the plate. They fell silent as they chewed the sweet treat that tasted like a mixture of pineapple and mango, with a hint of banana.

'None for me, thanks. I'm full,' Katie said with a contented sigh.

Mia seized both pieces and stuffed them into her mouth.

The family had feasted on a supper of freshly caught snapper and mashed yucca root, expertly cooked by James over the campfire. Now, as the sun went down, they could all relax.

Fleur glanced at her mum as she put her hands behind her head and settled back against a rock. Her round face was wreathed in smiles and her fair hair had grown to shoulder length. The cut-off jeans that she'd been wearing since Day 1 were badly frayed and she'd tied her pink shirt into a knot at the front – a style that showed off her bare brown midriff. Her prized flip-flops lay in the sand close to where she sat.

Busy clearing up the clam shell plates and coconut-shell bowls, James almost dropped one of the plates. Alfie lunged sideways to catch it before it landed. He handed it back to his dad then sauntered off to sit by himself on *Sandpiper II*, the unfinished raft that they'd started to build after fire had struck the camp and burned their first raft to ashes.

A tired Mia snuggled up beside Katie to enjoy a cuddle. 'Mum, do you have to go to Lookout Point tonight?' she asked through half-closed eyes. 'Can't you stay here with us?'

Katie gave her an extra squeeze. 'Someone has to keep the fire going at Lookout Point,' she reminded her. 'What if it went out and a ship sailed past Dolphin Island? They wouldn't know that we were here without the fire on the mountain to tell them, would they?'

'I can go if you like,' James offered as he washed the plates in a bowl made from a cut-down container. His dark hair and beard had grown curlier, and now that his cracked ribs had healed, he looked fit and relaxed.

Katie nodded. 'I'll put this tired girl to bed then.' She stood up and pulled Mia to her feet.

Fleur watched her mum lead Mia towards the shelter. Her younger sister's bed was furthest from the door; a simple wooden frame with woven palm fronds forming a shallow, comfy hammock. Nights could be cold here on the island but a blanket made from woven straw lined with downy feathers would help to keep her warm.

'A penny for them, Fleury?' James had finished with the dishes and was getting ready for his night shift at Lookout Point. He gave his pensive daughter a soft smile. She looked dreamy and faraway with her long brown hair falling in wispy ringlets, her freckled face lit up by warm, flickering firelight, long legs drawn up towards her chin.

She shook her head.

'Not worth a penny, eh?'

'I was just wondering – do you think Alfie's OK?' Though it was typical of her brother to wander off by himself, she knew that it often meant that he was feeling more homesick than usual.

James glanced in his son's direction. 'Why not go and find out?'

So Fleur stood up and went to sit beside Alfie in the dark shadow of a group of tall palms. Her arrival sent the two monkeys squealing and chattering higher up the cliff face. 'You OK?' she asked quietly.

'Yep. Don't want to talk though.'

'OK, we can just sit. Shift along.'

He made room for her on the raft. Together they gazed out to sea, watching a pale, almost full moon rise in the delicate pink sky. The light would soon fade, bringing velvety blue darkness. Waves would break against the two rocky headlands bordering their bay, a never-ending, restless rush of background noise that filled their heads wherever they went.

'Seven and a half weeks,' Alfie said at last. The waves crashed, the moon rose bright silver.

'Let's do some more work on *Sandpiper* tomorrow,' Fleur suggested after another long silence. 'If we stick at it, we can finish her in a couple of days.' The bamboo platform was built but the raft still needed the tricky finishing touches of mast and sails. 'After that, we can sail on her as far as Misty Island to the south and try to make contact with the outside world.'

Alfie shook his head then confessed his secret dread. 'The current's too strong. I don't reckon we'd make it past Mangrove Bay.'

'Don't say that!' Fleur stood up and walked swiftly to the water's edge.

Alfie followed her. 'Sorry,' he mumbled.

'No problem.' Secretly she thought he might be right. After all, Alfie was the one who'd tried to sail *Sandpiper* away from the island, so only he knew how strong the currents were and how the waves and the wind could suddenly rise and capsize you, crack your mast and tear down the sails.

Water swirled around their ankles as they looked out towards the black reef. 'I miss our house,' he confessed. 'I miss going to school. I miss my mates.'

'And Grandma and Granddad,' she added.

'Plus, I hate scorpions and hurricanes. I hate going into the jungle.'

'Me too.' An involuntary shudder ran down her spine as she glanced up at the mountain.

'I hate sharks.'

'Likewise.'

Alfie turned to Fleur and looked her in the eye as he voiced his deepest fear. 'Most of all, I hate thinking we might never go home.'

*

Fleur woke next morning to find George perched on her shoulder. Her bandy-legged, scaly-skinned friend flicked out his long tongue in hungry anticipation.

'Hiya, George. Sorry, I haven't got any breakfast for you,' she whispered, careful not to stretch her arms and disturb her pet gecko while the rest of the family slept on. It was scarcely light; surely too early for her to get up.

George kept on staring.

'Oh, OK – you win,' she sighed after a while. She sat up slowly and felt him scuttle down her back on to her bed and from there on to the wooden floor then out of the shelter on to the sand. When Fleur followed him, she found that the campfire was low so she fetched logs and branches from the wood store and placed them on to the glowing embers. A glance up the cliff face to Lookout Point told her that James had kept his fire going through the night. 'What would you like to eat?' she asked George as they made their way to the food store – a deep fissure in the rock topped with a heavy slab of stone to keep out marauding monkeys. She shifted the slab to one side and pulled out some pieces of shelled coconut. 'Shall I cut this up into tiny pieces for you?'

George ran up on to her shoulder once more. He licked at the white flesh, flicked his long green tail then turned away.

'No good?' Fleur watched as he ran down her arm and jumped on to a rocky ledge where he unfurled his tongue and curled it around an unsuspecting spider. Within a split second the juicy morsel had been gobbled up. *Yum!*

While nimble George scaled the rock in search of a second helping of arachnid, she peered into the store and decided that there were enough gulls' eggs for one more meal. They would go nicely with crab meat for breakfast, she decided. So she set off for the headland separating Base Camp Bay from Echo Cave Beach, carrying an empty plastic bag and two big clam shells that she would use to scoop crabs out of the water. Her plan was to fill the bag with tasty crabs and return in triumph before her mum, Mia and Alfie had woken up.

She hadn't got far, however, when Alfie emerged from the shelter, his hair tousled from sleep.

'Wait for me,' he called as he followed her. 'Are you going for a swim?'

'No, I'm going crabbing. You still want to come?'

He shrugged then nodded.

'You're feeling better then?'

'Yeah. Sorry.' The start of a new day always brought fresh hope, along with more beachcombing, fruit collecting and fishing. And, if they were lucky, more swimming with Pearl, Jazz and Stormy. He ran a hand through his spiky hair and grinned sheepishly.

'That's OK.' Fleur reached the headland and began to climb. She knew that they would find the rock pools teeming with marine life: silver tiddlers too small to eat, clusters of jellyfish with nasty stings, prickly anemones that clung to the wet rock and hopefully decent-sized crabs scuttling between pools or hiding under rocks.

Fleur and Alfie picked their way with care. A cool breeze blew in off the water and a golden-red sun crept up from behind the mountain peak. A few storm petrels fluttered up and away from the headland, followed by a single black cormorant that took off and flapped lazily across the bay. Fleur noticed that its black plumage had a beautiful greenish tinge.

'I wonder what cormorant eggs taste like,' Alfie said.

His idle remark brought her back to the task in hand. 'Never mind that for now. Let's start looking for crabs.' She secured the plastic bag under a rock then crouched beside the nearest pool to lift a loose rock. 'Nothing,' she reported. 'Try that one over there.'

Alfie lifted a second rock to reveal two starfish and an anemone. A third rock hid nothing except a startled striped parrotfish that shot out from its hiding place then, with a quick flick of its tail, darted into a narrow fissure out of harm's way.

Meanwhile Fleur moved on to the next pool which was deeper than the first. She went down on her knees and stared into the clear water. 'Wow!' she mouthed, before reaching in and drawing out a large, empty conch shell. She tipped it upside down with both hands and let the salt water trickle out. Light brown and knobbly on the outside, its curving inside lip was pearly white shot through with bright pink. Fleur turned it this way and that, felt its weight and ran her fingers along the perfectly smooth interior.

'I thought we were meant to be catching crabs,'

Alfie reminded her as he came to stand beside her.

'We will – soon,' she promised. She'd never seen such a beautiful conch specimen. The shell was at least twenty-five centimetres long, perfect in every way.

'Try blowing into it,' he suggested. Something about the shape of a conch meant that you were supposed to be able to blow into the narrow end and produce a sound like a trumpet.

Fleur put the conch to her lips and blew. She made a damp, spluttering noise then drew a deep breath and tried again. This time the shell gave a narrow squeak.

'Here, let me have a go.' Alfie had an idea of how to purse his lips before blowing. He took the heavy shell, tilted his head back, pressed his lips hard against the cold, wet surface and blew with all his might.

Fleur watched him blow out his cheeks like a puffer fish. She heard with astonishment the shrill, high note that came out of the pearly shell. 'Wow!' she breathed.

Alfie gave it a second go. The note was deeper and louder. It echoed around the bay.

Mia came running out of the shelter in her dad's big

white T-shirt that she wore as a nightie. Still half asleep, Katie emerged more slowly.

'That was pretty impressive,' Fleur murmured. 'Try again.'

Alfie grinned at her. He took another deep breath and produced two loud notes by stopping up the hole with his tongue before blowing again. The powerful sounds cut through the still air.

Mia had reached the headland and began to scramble over the rocks towards Alfie and Fleur. But she stopped a few metres short of where they stood and did a dance on the spot. 'Look, look, look!' she cried in delight.

Three dolphins swam swiftly into the bay. They cut through the calm water, only the tops of their round heads and their dorsal fins visible, but it was clear at a glance that Stormy led the way, ahead of Pearl and Jazz.

'They picked up the sound of the conch shell.' Fleur knew that dolphins had amazing hearing. They used their echolocation technique over great distances and picked up every sound. 'They must like the noise it makes!'

Alfie gave Fleur the shell then ran to the edge of the rocks. He waved both hands above his head. 'Yes. They've come to play.'

Sure enough, Stormy leaped out of the water, showing them his white belly and flapping his flippers against his sides. Then little Pearl sped alongside, giving Alfie her cheerful, birdlike whistle. She opened her mouth then clapped her jaws together and slapped her tail flukes on the water to make a huge splash. Fleur's Jazz came last. He made a spectacular leap high into the air, clean over the heads of Pearl and Stormy.

Alfie couldn't wait a second longer. He flung himself headlong from the headland into the sea.

Pearl was waiting for him as he rose to the surface through a cloud of bubbles and he threw both arms around her and laid his head against her flank where the shark bite had healed. She seemed to smile at him as she carried him away from the rocks.

'Wait for me and Stormy,' Mia yelled. She dived into the waves then came up and clambered straight on to her dolphin's back. Before she knew it she was riding rodeo-style through the waves.

Fleur glanced down at the conch shell, wondering if she could copy what Alfie had done. She put it to her lips, blew hard – and yes, she made a long, high note! Jazz rose on to his tail and did his funny tail-walk then spun round and threw himself backwards into the water. When he resurfaced, he blew a strong jet of water through his blowhole, deliberately soaking her with its spray.

'OK, I'm coming!' Fleur couldn't resist the invitation to join in. Placing the conch carefully on the ground, she took a running dive clear of the rocks.

Jazz greeted her with his two-note whistle – high-low, high-low – and a series of happy squeaks. He nudged her shoulder with his long lower jaw. *Be quick, climb up!*

Almost before Fleur knew it she was astride her dolphin's back and they had caught up with the others. The three were neck and neck as they sped out past the reef. They cut swiftly through the sparkling water out towards the rising sun, carrying their breathless passengers on a wild ride through the waves.

Back on shore, Katie climbed the headland then

picked up the conch shell and tucked it safely under her arm. From his vantage point high on the lookout ledge, James smiled as he watched his kids and the three young dolphins play.

Chapter Three

Mia borrowed Alfie's knife to cut a notch in the calendar stick. Day 54.

The upright stick was rammed into the sand close to the shelter entrance, bearing one notch for each day on the island. It was Mia's job to mark it and keep track of the days.

With hair still dripping-wet from their swim, she stood back, hands on hips, to admire the neatness of her work.

'Knife, please.' Alfie held out his hand and she passed it to him. The swim with Pearl had been the best possible start to the day so he was in high spirits as he used the whittled bone blade to scrape flesh from the crab shells that Katie had cooked. He scooped the steaming flesh on to a clam shell then offered the first helping to Fleur.

'Thanks for catching breakfast for us,' Fleur said to her mum as she used her fingers to gobble it up. 'I meant to do it before you woke up.'

Katie gave her a wink. 'But playing with Jazz got in the way?'

Fleur nodded happily. 'Did you see me stand on his back?' She'd balanced precariously, using him as a surfboard while he forged through the waves, and she'd lasted ten thrilling seconds before toppling into the water. 'Then he took me down to look at the fish swimming in the coral reef. I clung on to his fin while he dived really deep.'

'I'm glad you had fun.' Katie took her portion of crab meat. She watched Mia lift the heavy conch shell and struggle to put it to her lips, then laughed as she blew, spluttered and gasped.

'Why won't it make a proper sound?' Mia demanded crossly.

'Because it takes a lot of practice,' Alfie explained. 'Anyway, maybe we should make a new rule – we only blow the shell when we want Pearl and the others to come – not at any other time. It can be our new signal.'

33

'Good idea.' Fleur took the conch from Mia and set it down in the soft sand behind one of the stilts that supported the shelter. 'From now on this is its special place. No one moves it unless we want to use it to call Jazz, Stormy and Pearl.'

'No one moves what?' James asked as he scrambled down from the cliff path on to the beach.

Mia ran to him and gave him a hug. 'Hi, Dad. We're talking about our new conch shell. Come and look.'

'So that's what I heard from way up the mountain?'

'Yes. Alfie can play it. He's going to teach me.' Mia danced with delight as she showed him their new find.

Meanwhile, before she left for Lookout Point, Katie spread her fingers and counted off the jobs for the day: one – collect water, two – firewood, three – jackfruit, four – sugarcane, five – yucca roots …

'I plan to go over to Echo Cave Beach to see what the last storm threw up,' James decided. 'Who wants to come?'

'Me.' Mia immediately took off towards the headland without her hat.

'Slow down, Mi-mi.' Her dad picked up the hat

then set off after her. 'We've got plenty of time.'

'Water for me,' Fleur decided. 'And then jackfruit.'

'Yucca and maybe some bamboo canes.' Alfie knew exactly where to go for these – over the southern headland on to Turtle Beach and into the thick grove of bamboos growing at its fringe.

After a round of cheerful goodbyes they split off in different directions. Fleur hummed a tune as she climbed the cliff path. Today, there was no one to complain at her for pausing to examine a blue moon butterfly sunning itself on a broad green leaf or to pick up a peacock feather and stick it into her hatband or to stand and enjoy the sight of the eclectus parrot pecking at seeds on the ground. Its red and purple plumage told her that it was a female. Eager to find out how tame the bird might be, Fleur advanced slowly.

The parrot stopped pecking to raise her head and train her bright yellow eyes on Fleur who promptly dipped into the pocket of her denim shorts and pulled out a small piece of dried jackfruit. She crouched down and offered it to the bird. The suspicious parrot was eventually overcome by curiosity. She lowered her

head, picked up her feet and stepped gingerly towards the slice of fruit. Fleur didn't move, though the hooked beak and sets of claws looked super-sharp. Closer and closer the parrot came, until at the very last moment she darted her head forward and sank her beak into the jackfruit.

Fleur gasped and pulled her hand away just in time. The parrot seized the fruit then spread her wings and flew off, high up the mountain towards the jungle.

Not very tame after all. Fleur didn't fancy having her fingers nipped by that vicious-looking beak. She decided instead to concentrate on reaching the waterfall and filling the two containers that she carried with her.

But there were so many distractions for a budding naturalist. She stopped again to watch an albatross, the most spectacular of seabirds, wing its way across Base Camp Bay. Huge and mysterious! Could it really be true that killing an albatross was seen as a bad omen? Sailors of old thought so. They lived in dread of the cry of 'Albatross!' from the boy up in the crow's nest. If the bird came to harm, then danger, disaster and death by drowning were bound to follow.

But that was a silly superstition. Fleur tried to shake such thoughts from her head and climbed on. Approaching Butterfly Falls at last, she submerged the containers under the fast-running stream and enjoyed the sensation of cold water splashing on to her wrists.

There were many superstitions surrounding the sea, she realized. Setting sail on a Friday was supposed to be unlucky for a start. And mariners used to be afraid of mythical Sirens luring them on to rocks with their beautiful songs.

You shouldn't even whistle on a ship in case it strengthened the wind and brought bad luck.

It was weird how superstitions stuck with you, especially when you were alone. The albatross was already well out of sight and there were no women's voices singing above the sound of the waves that broke on the shore below. Nothing bad was about to happen.

To convince herself of this, Fleur screwed the tops on to the full containers and set herself another task. Judging the position of the sun in the sky, she worked out that she had time to climb to Lookout Point before its energy-sapping rays forced her to take a rest. She would stop there for a quick chat with her mum then carry on up the steep slope towards the edge of the jungle to pick up ripe jackfruit from the ground.

Good plan, she thought, leaving the containers by the waterfall and heading up the bare lower slopes of the mountain. To her surprise she didn't find Katie at Lookout Point. Perhaps she'd gone searching for firewood at the edge of the jungle and Fleur would meet her on her way down. Sweating under the dazzling sun, she slogged her way up the mountain towards its tree-covered peak.

There was still no sign of Katie, but a dozen monkeys ran out of the trees, tumbling head over heels in their hurry. *What's wrong? What are you running away from?* Fleur stopped to rest and wipe sweat from her forehead. The macaques chattered and shrieked as they sprinted down the hill. *Where are you, Mum?*

In spite of the fierce heat, Fleur felt a sudden shiver run down her spine. Was the monkeys' flight linked to the terror that she, Alfie and Mia felt in the jungle? They couldn't help but feel that a mystery Creature lurked in its leafy depths – a fear that Fleur must now fight hard to block. But try as she might, a sense of dread pounded at her ribs.

Suddenly she was surrounded by monkeys. They slid past her down the gravel slope, raising a cloud of red dust and dislodging small rocks. They bared their teeth and clutched at the sparse grass and low bushes on their way down to Lookout Point where they skidded to a halt and regrouped to draw breath.

Fleur bit her bottom lip then forced herself to glance up towards the jackfruit trees at the edge of the jungle. She saw a flash of pink and then her mum emerged from the black shadows, dragging a heavy branch.

'Mum! Mum! There you are!' *At last!* Relief made Fleur's head spin and she almost sank to her knees.

'Hi, Fleury. Can you give me a hand with this wood for the fire?'

Pull yourself together, Fleur told herself. *Forget about stupid secrets and superstitions. There isn't a scary Creature in the jungle.* 'Sure thing,' she yelled to Katie as she hurried on.

*

'What do you think of these?' Alfie was the last to return home after the morning's expeditions. Fleur had said goodbye to her mum at Lookout Point then brought water and jackfruit to camp, their dad had collected useful objects like rope and more large clam shells from Echo Cave, but Alfie was convinced that he'd brought back the find of the day so he invited everyone to gather round.

Mia inspected the three greyish-brown, roughly spherical objects that he'd laid carefully on the sand. They had spiky green leaves sprouting from the side, with stringy roots growing from the bottom, and each was about the size of a small melon. 'What are they?' she asked with obvious disappointment.

'Yams,' Alfie told her proudly. 'They're like potatoes – you can cook and eat them.'

'Cool.' Fleur grinned at him. 'Where did you find them?'

'They were growing in among the yucca and sugarcane at the edge of Turtle Beach. There's plenty more to dig up when we've finished these.'

'Excellent, Alfie – well spotted.' Though the root

vegetables didn't look too exciting at first glance, James knew that they could be peeled, boiled then mixed with coconut and sugarcane to make an interesting new dessert. 'Or we can mix them with the jackfruit that Fleur found. Either way, they'll be nice and tasty.'

It had been a good morning's work. Fleur was determined not to tell the others about her sudden panic at the edge of the jungle. Why spoil the good mood by voicing her fears? And after all, the truth was that it had been their mum who had disturbed the macaques and sent them fleeing out of the jungle. So what would be the point?

'What's up? Are you in a bad mood?' Alfie inquired after she'd asked him for his knife and started to peel the smallest of the yams. He was busy boiling water in a dish fashioned from a car's hub-cap that he'd salvaged in Black Crab Cove. The rusty metal disc had been given a few strategic bashes with a heavy rock to make it more dish-shaped then filled with water and placed on the fire.

'No, I'm fine,' she answered with a forced smile. The

flesh of the yam was boringly pale and pasty. Still, she shared her dad's opinion that, once boiled and mixed with other ingredients, it might taste more interesting than it looked.

'No, you're not,' he said quietly.

'Yeah, I am. I'm fine.' She changed the subject by pointing to the morning's find: the conch shell stashed safely under the raised platform. 'When will you teach Mia how to blow it?'

'Dunno. Tonight, after supper maybe.' He watched her dice the vegetable. 'It depends if we want to give a signal to the dolphins.'

''Course we do. We'll be ready for another swim by then. They might be too far away to hear us though. By the way, I fed an eclectus parrot on my way up to the falls. It was a female.'

They tipped the yam into the boiling water and watched it cook.

'I'm hungry,' Mia called. She'd used the edge of a flat stone to mark out a hopscotch grid in the wet sand at the water's edge but she'd quickly grown tired of the game and came running up the beach. She went straight to the food store to pester her dad. 'What's for lunch? I hope it's not that yucky yammy stuff.'

'Don't call it yucky until you've tasted it.' James lifted out a coconut and two lengths of sugarcane. He handed her the coconut. 'Go and bash this against a rock,' he instructed. 'Catch the milk in a plastic container. Try not to spill any.'

Soon everyone was busy preparing a lunch of boiled gannets' eggs and mashed yucca root followed by the intriguing new pudding. They chatted as they worked then sat in a circle around the campfire to eat what they'd cooked.

'Well?' James asked when it came to the yam and coconut pudding course.

With their mouths full of the sweet mixture, Fleur and Alfie smiled and nodded.

He turned to Mia. 'Yucky or yummy?'

'Yu-umm-y!' she declared as she held her plate out for more.

Chapter Four

To survive on Dolphin Island the Fishers had created a strict regime. They got up as soon as it was light, had breakfast, then completed a list of chores before the sun rose too high in the sky. They never stayed out in the full noonday heat. Instead they took a siesta in the shade – either in the main shelter or in George's Cave closer to the water's edge. Later in the afternoon they went out to collect eggs or driftwood, or to do more fishing off the edge of the headlands. Any spare time was spent beachcombing or exploring, or, if they were lucky, swimming with the dolphins.

'My, my – two visits in one day!' Katie raised her eyebrows as she joined Mia, Fleur and Alfie on the shore to watch Pearl, Stormy and Jazz appear from behind the reef in the evening of Day 54. Light pink

45

clouds scudded across the dusk sky as a breeze came in from the east.

'We called them with this.' Mia held up the conch. 'Alfie showed me how to blow it.'

'Well done, Mi-mi. It's like using a smartphone – now you can talk to Stormy any time you want.'

Alfie grinned at the comparison. 'Except a conch doesn't fit in your pocket.'

'And there's no satellite signal,' Fleur added.

'That's a fair point.' Taking the shell from Mia, Katie smiled as she watched them dash into the water. These days they had no fear of the waves or the strong currents and they swam like fishes. And of course, the dolphins were there to help if anyone got into trouble. She heard James call her name and glanced up the beach to see him standing by the fire waving for her to come.

'I'm on my way,' she called back as she turned and walked contentedly up the beach. The Fishers of Dolphin Island had got safely through another day. The kids were healthy and happy. What more could a mother ask?

*

Pearl greeted Alfie by nudging his shoulder with her beak. He stroked the top of her head then swam alongside while Mia, excited as always, clambered on to Stormy's back and let out a yell as he carried her swiftly across the bay.

Pearl gave Alfie a second nudge. *Again!*

So he patted her and flung his arm around her smooth, muscular body. 'I know – having the conch is so cool!' he confided. 'I bet you can hear it from miles away.'

Close by, Fleur pretended to ignore the fact that her brother was talking to his dolphin as if Pearl understood every word he said. Grinning to herself, she used both palms to slap the water and make a big splash. The spray showered down on to Jazz. 'Gotcha!' she cried before Jazz whisked his tail and smacked it down on the surface, making a splash that was three times as big. 'Hey!' He did it again and then a third time until she was drenched. 'OK, you win!'

Meanwhile, Stormy took Mia on a joyride all the way around the reef then back again. When they rejoined the others, Fleur saw that Stormy held a long strand of green sea wrack in his clamped jaws.

'Oh look, he wants to play the seaweed game!' Fleur lunged at him and snatched the dripping strand. She tossed it high in the air and watched Pearl leap to catch it. It landed on her snout so she shook it off and let Jazz take it in his mouth then fling it sideways for Stormy to catch. 'Too slow!' she called as speedy Pearl intercepted it then carried it off between her jaws.

'Go get it, Stormy!' Mia bet Alfie that her dolphin could catch Pearl. Sure enough, he soon overtook her and grabbed one end of the seaweed. He tugged at it until it broke in two. *End of game. What next?*

'Hey, look at Jazz go!' Fleur trod water as Jazz put on a burst of speed then leaped clear of the water to perform a full spin in the air. He blew a loud raspberry through his lips then plunged back into the sea. A few seconds later he reappeared and cosied up to Fleur.

'Time for a ride?' she asked.

But instead of waiting for her to climb on board, Jazz swam behind her and nudged the soles of her feet. Mia and Alfie felt Stormy and Pearl line up to do the same thing.

'They want a race,' Fleur realized. 'We have to lie

flat. They're going to push us with their beaks.'

So they all lay belly-down with arms stretched straight ahead, ready to begin.

'On your marks, get set, go!' Mia cried.

They were off! The dolphins pushed from behind and Fleur, Alfie and Mia surged through the water, creating a small bow wave as they sped forward. They had to close their eyes as water whooshed into their faces.

Fleur laughed out loud while Alfie and Mia hollered at the tops of their voices. 'Faster!' they shouted. 'Go, Stormy! Go, Pearl!'

Fleur laughed so much that she forgot to hold her legs stiff. Her knees buckled and she collapsed under the water, leaving her and Jazz trailing behind. Then Mia and Stormy met an incoming wave. It curled over their heads and tipped Mia off course, leaving Alfie and Peal to ride its crest and come safely out the other side.

'Winners!' Alfie's yell of triumph echoed across the bay.

Mia and Fleur grabbed their dolphins' fins and let them carry them to the headland where Alfie and Pearl waited. Before they knew it, they were swimming below the surface amongst a shoal of silversides – hundreds and hundreds of the tiny, glittering fish in a silent world of pink coral and swaying sea grass.

They stayed under until it felt as if their lungs would burst. Then they let go of Stormy, Pearl and Jazz and swam to the surface, towards the sunlight. They gasped and sucked in air then dived under a second time to see their dolphins glide gracefully between reef pinnacles, through clefts in dark rock, in amongst dainty yellow angelfish, translucent jellyfish, slow, grey groupers and slithery eels. Twenty, thirty, forty seconds – Fleur, Alfie and Mia stayed under for as long as they could hold their breaths. Then up again, kicking hard, cleaving through the clear water, followed by the dolphins so that they all reached the surface together. Jazz blew hard through his blowhole, high into the air. Stormy gave a shrill whistle. Pearl blew a raspberry with her upturned mouth. *Goodbye. Goodbye. Goodbye.*

It was time to go. Turning towards the horizon, the playful dolphins set off to join the rest of their pod, waiting patiently beyond the reef. They departed in a cloud of bubbles, leaping and clearing the water in wonderful, athletic arcs, speeding away.

*

'We're nearly out of firewood.' It was Alfie who made the discovery when he went to the wood store on Lookout Point early next morning. 'Fleur, did you hear me? I said – we need more wood.'

'Uh?' Something much more interesting than firewood had caught Fleur's attention. She sat on the long stone ledge with her back to him, observing a red and purple parrot perched on a thin branch in a nearby myrtle bush. The parrot shifted her weight from side to side, as if deciding whether or not to hop down and join her.

'The fire's going out,' he warned crossly.

The parrot dipped her head and gave a short squawk. She raised her wings in preparation for flight.

'Hiya. Are you the same one as yesterday?' Fleur murmured, sliding her fingers into her pocket in the hope of finding something that a parrot might like to eat. 'It'd be good if I had some more jackfruit.'

Alfie strode across the ledge towards her. 'Fleur, why aren't you listening to me?'

The sudden movement scared the parrot and she launched herself noisily from the bush, flapping away across the open scrubland to the west.

'Spoilsport!' Fleur turned with a disgusted frown. 'I could've tamed her if you'd kept quiet. She could've been a pet.'

'You've already got George. Anyway, we don't need more pets. We need firewood.' He gestured towards the dying fire.

'Oh, OK – you win.'

'Now. We need it now!'

They'd been sent up the mountain with the usual instruction to keep the fire going but they'd taken their time and done other stuff on the way. Alfie had sat on a rock and gazed out to sea for a long time, hoping as always for a sighting of his favourite mammal – just a second or two of dolphins swimming along the horizon would have been enough, watching them go about their daily business of catching fish and squid. Fleur, meanwhile, had been distracted by a pale blue butterfly she'd never seen before and by a different species of bat to the mouse-tailed variety she'd spotted the day before.

'Sorry. I guess we'd better get a move on.' Reluctantly she left the ledge and set off up the mountain, crossing a few hundred metres of shale and scrubland before turning to check that Alfie was keeping up. The way ahead grew steeper and rockier and the dark jungle gave off its usual sense of mystery. 'Let's hope we can pick up some dead branches without going too far in,' she muttered.

'What did you say?' In his haste he slipped and skidded but he finally caught her up.

'We need to find wood under the jackfruit trees. I don't fancy going any further.'

'Yep, it'll be quicker if we don't have to. Anyway, I forgot my knife.' He needed it to cut through thick undergrowth and long lianas that looped down from the trees. 'We won't get anywhere without it.'

It was agreed – they would skirt the edge of the jungle. Both breathed sighs of relief then gritted their teeth and told themselves not to be chicken. After all, it was broad daylight.

They went on in sweltering heat and soon came to the spot where they hoped to find dead branches on the ground that they could drag down to Lookout Point. But their approach startled a possum in the nearest jackfruit tree. With limbs splayed and stretching out the thin flaps of skin between its legs, it glided from one tree branch to another, setting off a chain reaction amongst a group of squat, grey birds that emerged from the bushes and ran clumsily down the hill. The flightless bowerbirds were followed by a black-eared giant rat, as big as a cat, with a fat, pouchy belly and a long, thick tail.

Alfie jumped to one side as the rat scuttled close to his bare legs. 'Ugh!'

'What's wrong? It's only a squirrel without a bushy tail.' Fleur didn't understand his reaction.

'*Not!*' Alfie countered.

'Yes. They both belong to the rodent family ...' She stooped to pick up a decaying branch that was so wet and soggy that it fell apart in her hands. No good.

'I don't need a natural history lecture, thanks.'

The scratchy conversation continued as they moved

from tree to tree, putting ripe fruit to one side and searching in vain for suitable wood until at last Alfie stumbled across a neat heap of twigs and dry, brown leaves that looked as if it had been left there on purpose. The round pile was roughly half a metre high. 'Who did this?' he wondered aloud.

'Or *what* did it?' Fleur moved in for a closer look. She crouched down and poked it with a stick, half expecting a small creature to spring out from its carefully constructed hiding place. But nothing moved and so she poked again.

'Careful!' Alfie warned. He stood at a safe distance, bent forward with his hands on his knees to brace himself in case something did jump out. 'Maybe we should leave it?' he suggested.

But Fleur was on a mission to solve the mystery. Placing the stick on the ground, she began to lift the twigs and brush away the leaves until she came to a mound of gritty sand. 'Some creature went to a lot of trouble to camouflage this heap of dirt,' she said slowly. 'I wonder why.'

Alfie glanced over his shoulder at the shadowy mass

of tall, dark trees. In the thick, hot silence, he had a creepy sensation that something was watching them.

'I'm going to find out,' she decided as she eased the earth to one side. Eventually she touched something round and smooth. When she pressed the motionless object, she found that it gave way under her fingers. 'Weird – it's squidgy,' she murmured.

'Maybe …' he began again.

But Fleur took no notice. With light, sweeping motions, she scooped the grit away more rapidly until she revealed a grey, egg-shaped object, then a second and a third. In the end she exposed twenty of them – each the size of an ostrich egg, packed closely together in a carefully excavated hollow.

Alfie grimaced. 'Why are their shells soft? What are they?'

She glanced up at him with a worried expression. 'They could be lizard eggs.'

The explanation didn't seem too scary so Alfie's thoughts turned as usual to food. 'Can we eat them?'

'No. We'll leave them to hatch.' As swiftly as she'd exposed the eggs, Fleur covered them up again. 'They have to incubate first. I wish I hadn't disturbed them in the first place.'

'I told you not to.'

'I know you did. But I had no idea what was here.' Dismayed that she'd dug up the reptile nest, Fleur rebuilt the mound of twigs and leaves, taking care to leave it as she'd found it.

Alfie tutted. When he glanced back down the mountain to Lookout Point, his eyes widened and he let out a long groan. 'Oh no, we're in dead trouble. We've let the fire go out.'

Fleur's heart sank as she saw the last faint wisps of smoke rising from a heap of grey ashes. 'I'll say it was my fault,' she said in a subdued voice. 'I should've concentrated on fetching firewood.'

'We both should.' Alfie and Fleur had been too casual and now they'd really let everyone down. But there was nothing else for it – they would have to walk straight down to base camp and confess.

Chapter Five

'Never mind. What's done is done.' One quick look at Fleur and Alfie's dejected faces told James that they'd probably punished themselves enough.

Standing under the awning of their shelter, Fleur looked down at the sand, clasping her hands together and shifting her weight uncomfortably from one foot to the other. 'We're really sorry, Dad. We didn't let the fire go out on purpose.'

Mia slipped in between Fleur and a silent, red-faced Alfie. 'Mum will get it going again, won't she, Dad?'

Alfie wished that the ground would swallow him up as he remembered the deep frown on his mother's face after they'd arrived back at base camp and she'd listened to their confession before striding into the shelter to fetch the precious lens salvaged from a pair of broken glasses that they'd found on the beach. She hadn't said a word as she'd set off up the cliff path to relight the fire.

'Yes, she will,' James told Mia. 'She'll start it with a little pile of dried grass and some twigs. That's what she wants the lens for – to make the sun's rays really, really hot. But she'll need plenty more wood to keep the fire going once it's restarted.'

Mia ran to the wood store and lifted a piece of driftwood from the pile. 'I can take this up for her!'

James nodded. 'Good idea, Mi-mi. You and I will carry some wood from here up to Lookout Point. Alfie and Fleur, you go on a firewood-finding expedition to Turtle Beach. Bring back as much as you can carry.'

They nodded miserably.

'Wear your hats. Take plenty of water with you.'

'Will do.' Alfie went inside for his hat. He put two bottles of water into a plastic bag, tucked his knife into his waistband then went back out. 'Ready?' he asked Fleur, who nodded.

Without speaking, they set off across the hot sand. They were heavy-hearted as they climbed over the headland and descended on to the neighbouring beach where they began their search. While Alfie walked purposefully towards the stand of bamboos growing at the base of the cliff to see what he could find, Fleur poked her toe into a mound of seaweed left behind by the most recent high tide. Black flies buzzed around the rotting heap and she turned up plenty of rusty cans and an old bicycle tyre but nothing that could be used as firewood. She changed tack and headed on along the curving shoreline until she came across something that was ideal for burning, namely a panel of garden fence that had been flung on to the shore and lodged itself under a large rock. It was a decent find so she called to Alfie for help. 'This is stuck under the rock,' she yelled. 'I need help.'

He left what he was doing and ran to join her.

The fencing was well and truly jammed. 'Grab this free end and we'll pull together,' Fleur instructed. 'Once it's dried out, it should burn really well.'

They used all their strength but it wouldn't budge so Alfie dug around the base of the rock, scooping out handfuls of wet sand while Fleur jiggled the panel to loosen it. At last it started to move.

'Almost!' Fleur took a breather. She pushed her hair back from her forehead and turned towards the sea to let the breeze cool her face.

Alfie went on digging. *How had this piece of fence got here*? he wondered. It belonged in somebody's back garden with roses climbing up it, not on an uninhabited island in the middle of nowhere. How many thousands of miles had it travelled across oceans before it ended up here, amongst the tin cans, plastic bags and old car number plates? 'Try now,' he told Fleur as he rested back on his haunches.

She pulled again, gradually easing the panel from under the rock then overbalancing and falling backwards as, with a last jerk, it finally came free. She let go and landed flat on her back with her legs in the air. The fence toppled against the rock.

Alfie gave a yelp of laughter. 'Ha! You look like an upside-down turtle trying to turn the right way up.'

'Not funny!' She picked herself up and rescued her hat. 'Honestly, Alfie!'

He couldn't help himself. He bent forward and laughed until his stomach hurt.

'N-O-T, *not* funny!'

'You should have seen your face!' Mimicking her shocked expression, he sprang to his feet then ran off towards the water.

'You just wait!' She threatened to choke him with her bare hands if she managed to catch him.

'Oh no, you don't!' He felt her draw level and turned to fight her off, both ignoring the swelling wave that rolled towards them.

'Aagh!' Fleur cried as it crashed on to the shore and swept them both off their feet.

'Serves you right!' Fleur cried as the water closed over their heads. They resurfaced about twenty metres out and had to swim strongly for the shore before the next wave broke.

'Quick, our fence is floating away!' Alfie warned Fleur of the danger and they sprinted up the beach just in time to drag it clear of the water then flop down on the sand to recover.

'OK, no more fooling around,' Fleur decided as soon as she'd got her breath back. 'We have to get this back to base.'

They were about to set off for home when Alfie stopped to pick up a green plastic parcel cast up by the last wave. He weighed it in his hands then turned it this way and that. The parcel was tightly sealed and tied with string.

Fleur was as curious as he was. 'I wonder what's inside.'

'I haven't a clue. Do you want me to open it now or save it until later?'

'Now,' she decided, despite her resolution to hurry back to camp with the fence panel. 'Fingers crossed it's something useful.'

So Alfie took out his knife and cut the string then slid the blade under the plastic to reveal a layer of bubble wrap and some neatly folded contents. He lifted one corner with a puzzled frown.

'Here – give it to me.' Fleur was excited as she peeled back the bubble wrap and discovered more brightly coloured cotton items – lemon-yellow, lime-green and strawberry-pink, in fact all the colours of the rainbow. She took out the top one and held it up. 'T-shirts,' she breathed. 'Wow, Alfie – brand-new

T-shirts!' They were plain, everyday garments but Fleur couldn't have been happier if a designer dress had landed in her lap.

'Wowser.' At first he didn't sound too excited. 'It's lucky the plastic was watertight.'

She tugged at the front of the faded blue and white striped T that she'd been wearing for weeks. 'Now I can throw this old thing away and wear the lime-green one.' No sooner said than she'd pulled the new top over her head and was parading up and down the beach with a supermodel strut. 'How do I look?'

'Yeah, pretty good.' A new, clean T-shirt would be cool, he conceded.

'Mia can choose whatever colour she likes.'

Happy that Fleur was happy, Alfie placed the parcel on top of the fence panel and told her to pick up one end. 'Now it's back to base without stopping,' he insisted. 'Otherwise we'll land in big trouble twice in one day.'

*

It had been hard work, but by the end of the day Alfie and Fleur had found enough wood on Turtle Beach and then on Pirate Cave Beach to keep both fires going for at least twenty-four hours. The fence panel had been by far their best discovery, but they'd also found an old deckchair and part of a window frame, besides the usual pieces of bleached and dried-out driftwood that they'd added to their stores. As the sun began to sink behind the mountain and turn the sky a flaming red, they took Mia with them to carry the last load up to their mum on Lookout Point.

'Good job!' Katie greeted them with her wide smile followed by a hug. 'Now sit down and have a rest. You deserve one.'

With the newly lit, well-fed fire crackling away at the far end of the ledge and the smell of wood smoke in their nostrils, they perched side by side with their legs dangling over the edge, looking at the red sun's rays falling across the sea. Mia had chosen the zingy yellow T while Alfie had settled for bright orange – all colours that stood out in the gathering dusk.

'A hard day, huh?' Katie asked.

They nodded.

'But all's well that ends well.'

'Yeah,' Alfie said with a tired sigh. He glanced round at the mountain slope. 'Hey, Fleur – we didn't tell Mum about the dinosaur eggs yet.'

Mia's eyes widened. 'Dinosaur?' she echoed, caught between fear and excitement. 'Where?'

'Not really a dinosaur.' Fleur gave him a warning glance. 'Alfie's only kidding.'

Katie put a comforting arm around Mia's shoulder. 'So what are we talking about?' she asked Fleur.

'Actually, lizard eggs.'

'A lizard like George?' Mia wanted to know.

'Yes, but bigger.' Fleur still felt guilty about disturbing the nest and was reluctant to go into details.

'Much bigger,' Alfie added. 'Huge actually. The eggs were hidden under a heap of leaves and dirt. Fleur dug right down and found lots of them. It made me wonder, what kind of lizard lays ones like that?'

'Plenty.' Fleur was ready with the answer. 'George is tiny, but some adult geckos grow half a metre long. They would lay pretty big eggs for a start. Or iguanas maybe.'

'But not dinosaurs?' Mia had learned about them

from scary films so she didn't fancy meeting one on Dolphin Island.

'No, Mi-mi. They're extinct. They died out millions of years ago.' Katie saw that her youngest daughter's eyelids were drooping and decided it was time to pack her off to bed. 'I bet Monkey's waiting for you in that nice cosy shelter. Why not go and find out?'

'I'll come with you.' Alfie stood up and offered to lead the way.

'And I'll stay here,' Fleur decided.

'No, Fleury – you go with them. You know how fast it gets dark once the sun goes down.' Katie had noticed a bank of thick clouds gathering on the horizon. 'Besides, I think it's going to rain tonight. Best get back to base camp before it starts. Have a good sleep and wake up bright-eyed and bushy-tailed, ready to begin a brand-new day.'

*

There was no rain after all. And though there was hardly any wind, clouds drifted in off the sea and a thick, clammy mist settled over base camp. The night was long and dark.

Alfie lay awake, listening to the muffled sound of waves breaking on the rocks. At around midnight he crept outside to check the fire. It was still burning steadily so he retreated into the shelter and tried once more to get to sleep. The trouble was, he couldn't stop thinking gloomy thoughts. What would happen, for instance, if one of the family got sick again, like Fleur had with tick-bite fever? Or if someone had an accident and broke a bone? Or if, for some unknown reason, they ran out of food? Or if Pearl, Stormy and Jazz never visited them again? This last idea made him so miserable that he got off his bed and went outside again where he sat cross-legged by the fire, staring into the mist.

'Alfie?' An unhappy voice broke the silence.

He turned and made out Mia standing in the doorway, clutching Monkey. 'What's wrong, Mi-mi?'

'I had a bad dream.'

'Come and sit here with me.' He waited for her to join him. 'What was it about?'

'The Creature,' she whimpered. The firelight illuminated her tear-stained face.

'You mean the one you saw in the jungle that time?'

Mia nodded.

'Oh, Mi-mi – I thought you'd forgotten about that.'

'Me too.' She did try to, but sometimes memories came flooding back while she was sleeping. Daytime was mostly OK – there was always plenty to do – but as soon as it got dark she would relive the time in the forest when she'd got lost. She'd glimpsed the Creature's big teeth and long claws between the bushes and screamed and run and tripped and fallen into the mud. Fleur had found her and led her out of the tangle of creepers and tall trees into the sunlight.

'I have bad dreams once in a while,' Alfie confessed. 'We all do.'

'What are yours about?'

'About being shipwrecked. In my nightmare I'm back on *Merlin* and the storm is beginning all over again. I think the boat's heading for the rocks and I'm hanging on to her guardrail so as not to fall overboard. But the waves are too big. Then I'm in the sea and trying to swim but I can't stay afloat. That's when I wake up and, guess what, it turns out everything's all right. I'm here on Dolphin Island. There's no storm or waves or rocks. I'm safe.'

'That's what I do,' Mia said eagerly. 'I dream the Creature's following me, hissing and stamping and swishing its tail. I run away but it's catching up with me, it's getting closer, opening its mouth and I can see its sharp teeth. Then I'm awake and I start to cry.'

'And there's nothing there after all.' He patted her hand. 'Just me, Fleur and Mum and Dad.'

'And Monkey,' she whispered as she hugged him to her.

The flames flickered orange and the embers glowed bright red. Dark mist swirled across the beach. On the mountain a group of macaques gave their high, chattering call and out beyond the headland a pod of dolphins swam silently by.

Chapter Six

'Avast! Raise the anchor, man the mainsail – we're off!' Alfie rallied the ship's crew.

'Avast!' Mia laughed. Shrugging off the nightmare of the night before, she was eager to play pirates with him and Fleur, ready to set off for a day's beachcombing that would turn their daily chore into a big adventure.

'All shipshape?' Fleur checked Mia's outfit – worn-out trainers with holes in, frayed shorts, new yellow T-shirt and straw hat with feathers. 'I've got the water and sugarcane. Plus the conch shell, just in case.' She tapped the home-made rucksack hanging from her shoulder.

'Knife.' Alfie patted his belt. 'Now, Able Seaman Mia – check the rigging!'

'Aye, aye, Captain!' Mia was eager to reach Black

Crab Cove, which would mean trekking across Turtle Beach and Pirate Cave Beach until they came to the narrow cove surrounded by tall cliffs. There they would be able to explore the wreck of *Dolphin* again – the ancient wooden sailing ship that had run aground hundreds of years earlier. It was one of her favourite places on the whole island. So she led the way through the mist.

'Don't dash too far ahead,' Fleur called after her. 'We need to be able to see you.'

Alfie glanced up at the leaden sky. 'The day feels weird,' he commented. 'What's happened to the sun?'

'It's still up there somewhere.' Fleur hurried to catch up with Mia. Though she was only twenty paces ahead of them, she was hardly visible. 'At least there's no danger of getting sunburned.'

They settled in to the long walk ahead. 'If we find any useful stuff on the way, let's stash it in Pirate Cave.' Alfie had already picked up a piece of striped canvas – most likely from the old deckchair frame that he'd collected the day before. Meanwhile Mia came running back with a child's trainer that she'd found on the shoreline. The trainer was pink with glittery panels and white stripes.

'Is this any good?'

'Not unless we find the other one.' Fleur took the shoe, then they followed Alfie over the next headland.

'Watch out for jellyfish!' He'd almost put his foot on one stranded in a shallow rock pool. 'And barbed wire!' He was about to leave the coil of rusty wire where it lay but then had second thoughts. 'Maybe we can make use of this,' he muttered before adding it to his collection. He waited to show it to Fleur and Mia.

'What about these?' Mia had picked up two flat shells with a beautiful mother-of-pearl sheen on the underside. 'Keep or chuck?'

'Keep.' Alfie took them from her. 'Wait here. I won't be a minute.'

The girls watched him walk swiftly up Pirate Cave Beach and disappear into the mist.

Mia started to count. 'One second, two seconds, three seconds …'

Fleur spent the time trying to decide on the way ahead. It would be easy to lose their sense of direction unless they followed the shoreline. She took out a bottle of water and handed it to Mia.

'Fifty, fifty-one, fifty-two ...'

'Here I am.' Alfie returned empty-handed. 'I shoved everything under the boulder at the entrance to the cave.'

'Let's go.' Mia couldn't wait to get to the spot where *Dolphin* lay. She ran on again.

'Don't run too ... far ... ahead.' Fleur gave an exasperated sigh.

Alfie quickened his pace. 'Save your breath. Come on, let's catch her up.' By the time he and Fleur cleared the next headland into Black Crab Cove, Mia had spotted the wreck resting in the sand dunes at the base of the cliff and was sprinting up the beach on her thin sparrow-legs.

Alfie cupped his hands to his mouth. 'Ahoy, Able Seaman Mia, wait for your senior officers!'

'Aye, aye, Captain!' She stopped in her tracks and stood to attention.

Alfie grinned at Fleur. Together they walked up the unmarked white sand and gradually made out the shape of the upturned hull, its pale, rotting planks bleached by the sun, its old figurehead in the shape of a woman's head worn away by rain and wind. 'OK, Able Seaman, you have my permission to board *Dolphin*.'

'Yay!'

'A little rest would've been good,' Fleur grumbled. The clammy mist had drained her energy and her legs felt tired after the long trudge through soft sand.

'No chance.' Alfie reached the base of the wreck to find that Mia had already scaled to the top and was perched on the curved hull.

'Mind you don't fall!' Fleur's warning came just as three pelicans rose from the cliff face. The ungainly, speckled birds flew close to Mia who ducked down and covered her head with her arms. They flapped on past Fleur and Alfie towards the sea – three ghostly shapes vanishing into the mist.

'Wait for me, you two.' The ugly birds had given Mia a fright and she slid down on her bottom until she reached a point where she could safely jump on to the sand. She landed between Fleur and Alfie. 'Everything looks weird without the sun,' she said in a worried voice.

Fleur agreed. In the dim grey light it was easy to imagine ghosts of dead sailors haunting the decaying ship. She could almost hear their voices crying out as *Dolphin* came to grief in a terrific storm, then the splintering sound of the mast breaking and the dull crunch of the wooden hull against the deadly rocks.

'Never mind. This will cheer you up.' Alfie took the

conch out of Fleur's rucksack. 'Guess what?'

'Yay, we can call the dolphins!' Mia's mood changed in the blink of an eye. She snatched the shell from him. 'Let's go, let's go!'

Off she ran without a backwards glance until she came to the foot of the rock archway leading into Mangrove Bay. The unusual formation soared ten

metres into the air then arched back down to meet other pinnacles of rock worn down by breaking waves. Currents swirled in foaming eddies and spray rose high above her head – a dangerous but spectacular sight.

'Go ahead, Mia, blow the conch,' Alfie said when he joined her by Magic Arch. 'See what happens.'

She pressed the shell to her lips and blew hard. There was a squeak and then a splutter. 'You try,' she told Alfie the expert.

He shaped his lips then blew into the conch. A long, sweet note floated through the air.

They waited for a while. 'Again,' Mia told him. It would make her day if Stormy appeared through the mist, swimming under the arch and greeting her with his high whistle.

He tried a second time.

'Nothing.' Fleur shook her head. 'Maybe the sea's too rough for them to come close to shore.'

'It's been loads rougher than this and they've still showed up,' Alfie reminded her.

'So maybe there's a storm further out to sea.'

Something was making their dolphins stay away. 'Or maybe they're sleeping.'

'You said dolphins don't sleep.' Mia jutted out her bottom lip.

'They do, but only with half of their brain.' On the whole, Fleur decided that her theory about a bad storm out to sea was the answer. 'Sorry, Mi-mi. We're as disappointed as you are.'

Alfie lowered the conch and took one last look out to sea. The same three pelicans winged their way under the arch, swooping low and almost brushing their wings against the rock. As for Pearl, Stormy and Jazz – no sign.

*

A dejected Mia, Alfie and Fleur retraced their steps back to base camp, only stopping to collect the debris from Pirate Cave on the way. Alfie was careless as he reached under the boulder to drag out the coil of barbed wire. 'Ouch!' He'd stabbed his finger on one of the spikes and drawn blood so he wiped it on his new T-shirt. 'I don't even know what we can use this for.'

He was about to ditch the coil at the foot of the

cliff when Fleur took it from him. 'Let's take it. You never know.'

On they went with heads down and shoulders drooping. They were tired, hungry and frustrated but put on cheerful faces for their dad as they climbed the last headland and trudged up the beach.

'Hi, kids. Have you had a good day?' James said they should store their new finds under the palm trees. 'But not the shoe,' he said to Mia with a cheerful wink. 'Why not try it on and see if it fits?'

'Why? What's the good of her wearing one trainer?' Alfie objected. 'Even if it's the right size, she can't very well hop everywhere.'

'Why not? It might slow her down a bit,' Fleur muttered under her breath.

'Wait right there.' James disappeared into the shelter and came back out holding up the matching shoe. 'Look what I found this afternoon on Echo Cave Beach.'

'No way!' Mia grabbed the sparkly trainer and put it on. 'Look, it fits!'

'Yes way,' James said with a satisfied grin. 'Cinderella,

you *shall* go to the ball!'

*

For two days the mist didn't shift. It shrouded the mountain and dampened the mood of the whole family who went about their daily chores with serious faces. On the Monday, Day 57, they heard not one but two planes pass overheard. The first was early in the morning, as Mia was marking the calendar stick and Fleur and Alfie fished for crabs on the headland. They all heard the distant engine but didn't stop what they were doing. After all, what was the point when the mist was so thick that you couldn't see more than ten metres ahead? The second time was in the afternoon when they were all up at Lookout Point. The engine was louder and for a few minutes they hoped that the plane would fly low enough to spot their fire.

Fleur fed the flames, held her breath and glanced up at the sky. 'Maybe there'll be a break in the clouds.'

'You wish!' They hadn't shifted for two days and Alfie knew it would take a miracle.

He was right – the steady drone of the plane's engines grew fainter until at last there was silence.

Worse was to come. That night the skies opened at last and rain began to pour down. Within minutes everything in base camp was soaked. Alfie woke to the sound of water running down the cliff and splashing on to the roof of the shelter.

Fleur was already awake, with George perched on her shoulder. 'Fire's gone out,' she reported in a whisper. 'I went and checked.'

Not again! He groaned as he peered out at the torrential rain. Sure enough, the campfire was a heap of hissing grey ash.

'Let's hope the roof holds.' She'd already felt a trickle of cold water down her back and imagined the palm leaf thatch sagging under the weight of the downpour. 'Much more of this and the whole thing could collapse.'

Mis-er-able. Alfie shook his head and sighed.

They sat out the night as Mia and James slept and by morning the rain had eased. Katie came down from Lookout Point to help clear up the mess. Luckily a deep overhang of rock had kept her fire alight. She'd carried a burning torch of twigs bound by a rag soaked in coconut oil down the cliff path to relight the fire at base camp.

'Keep calm and carry on,' James told everyone as he and Fleur climbed on to the shelter roof to mend the leaks.

To the sound of runnels of water trickling off the cliff face, Alfie and Mia dried their clothes by spreading them over bushes, then emptied the leaking food store.

'The dried fish isn't dry any more.' Alfie held up two small, soggy fillets by their tails. 'And the sugarcane's gone mushy.'

'Save what you can,' Katie told him doggedly.

'Well done, Mum,' Mia murmured as the new fire caught light. For once she didn't run off to play but stayed quietly in the camp. 'When will the fog go away?'

Yeah, when? Alfie wondered. He'd expected a breeze to blow in off the ocean after last night's rain but it hadn't happened. Instead, the mist seemed thicker than ever, the air more stale and muggy.

'Stand back, Mi-mi.' Katie fanned the small flames.

'Alfie, lend me your knife for a sec.' James's job for

the morning was to weave new palm fronds over the holes in the roof.

No one offered an answer to Mia's question about the fog. Instead they kept their heads down and worked silently on.

Chapter Seven

'What are you two doing?' Mia asked Fleur and Alfie as she bit into a chunk of dried jackfruit.

'Keeping calm and carrying on.' Fleur had taken her dad's advice to heart. 'There's no point in moping around, waiting for the mist to clear.'

'So we decided to make a sail for *Sandpiper II*.' Alfie laid out his length of salvaged deckchair canvas on the soggy sand.

Fleur gave a doubtful shake of her head. 'But is it big enough?' Ideally they needed a larger piece of fabric. 'Haven't we got any of that sailcloth left?'

'From *Kestrel*?' He shook his head. They'd rescued a large sheet of ripped sail from a cruising yacht that had run aground during a previous storm but they'd used it all on making hammocks and patching the shelter roof. 'This is the only thing we've got.'

'OK, it'll have to do.' Fleur folded it then carried it to the raft which they'd dragged down the beach to the water's edge, ready for her maiden voyage. It was almost finished – there was a large canister lashed to each corner of the platform as flotation aids and the mast was fixed in place, made from the straightest piece of timber they'd been able to find. All they had to do now was to tie the canvas to the mast and give her a test run in the calm water of Base Camp Bay.

Losing interest, Mia left Alfie and Fleur and ran back up the beach to sit by the campfire and play with Monkey.

'I'm not sure about this mast.' Fleur stepped on to the raft to test its strength. 'Will it stand up to rough seas?'

'This is only to see if she floats. We can try it without the sail if you like,' Alfie replied.

'You're right. Let's do that.'

Together they manoeuvred *Sandpiper II* into position. Her platform of bamboo canes meant she was surprisingly light and before long she was bobbing happily in the shallow water. Waves broke gently around the air-filled canisters and rippled towards Alfie and Fleur who stood ankle-deep observing her.

'Cool.' Alfie noted that the flotation aids held her well clear of the water. 'She's looking good.'

A larger wave lifted her and sent her careering towards them. The canisters scraped along the wet sand until the next wave dragged her back out to sea.

'Oops!' Alfie ran in after her. He grabbed one corner of the platform. 'Is the tide coming in or going out?'

'Going out. Hang on, I'm on my way.' Fleur waded waist-deep into the sea to help him. She felt the drag of the outgoing tide and found it hard to keep her balance. She stumbled then fell on to one knee, soaking her new T-shirt before regaining her feet. 'At least we've found out that there's no problem about her being able to float.'

'Whoa!' The tide pulled the raft into deeper water and he was forced to let her go. 'Sorry – I couldn't hold on,' he gasped.

Instead of bobbing gently, *Sandpiper II* now rocked on the suddenly choppy surface five metres from where they stood. 'We should have used a rope to moor her,' Fleur realized. 'We didn't think this through.'

'Too late.' He threw himself into the water and began to swim in a ragged crawl towards the raft.

'Alfie, come back.' This wasn't good – the pull of the ebbing tide was taking *Sandpiper II* much further out. She'd almost disappeared into the mist.

The waves grew bigger. He saw the next wave roll towards him, felt seaweed wrap itself around his legs then he was lost under a rush of cloudy seawater and bubbles. His head broke the surface and he gasped for air.

'Come back!' she cried again. A fresh current had taken hold of the raft and flung her in a new direction, towards the rocky headland. 'Alfie, it's not worth it. Let her go!'

In the gap between waves he saw that Fleur was right. *Sandpiper II* was way beyond his reach. At this rate, he'd be lucky if he made it back to the beach. 'OK, I'm on my way!' He struck out in back crawl the way he'd come.

Fleur's gaze was torn between her brother's painfully slow progress and the drifting raft. Every time his head vanished under a wave she held her breath. *Sandpiper II* was tossed ever closer to the sharp rocks. He inched towards dry land while the raft lurched towards disaster.

Alfie swam with all his might until his feet touched the seabed and he was able to stagger the last few metres. He let Fleur grab his hand and haul him clear, just in time to see the last of *Sandpiper II*.

She dipped violently towards the headland. The current spun her round and she rocked again. The white canisters scraped the headland. She was trapped between two rocks. The waves pounded her and broke her flimsy mast in two. She broke free, lurched on again until a killer wave smashed over her and she was lost.

*

Mia knew nothing about the latest disaster as she made her way up the beach towards the dim glow of the campfire. She scuffed her feet through the sand, admiring her new sparkly pink trainers as she went. *When will Stormy come back for a visit?* she wondered as she began looking for Monkey. Her mum and dad had set off on a beachcombing expedition to Mangrove

Bay, so they weren't around to help. First she looked in the shelter, then stood outside, wondering whether to retrace her steps and search in George's Cave. 'Hi, George. I didn't see you.'

Fleur's gecko hung upside down from the awning. His bulging yellow eyes stared down at her.

'I've lost Monkey. I'm bored. What can I do?'

He didn't move.

'It's OK for you,' Mia grumbled. 'You can play with other geckos any time you like.'

Suddenly she remembered when and where she'd left Monkey – the previous day, up at Lookout Point. Without a second thought and forgetting all about the strict never-go-anywhere-by-yourself rule, she set off quickly for the cliff path. She didn't care if the fog made it hard to find her way – she definitely needed to find him.

*

'Nothing we can do.' Fleur felt her stomach twist in a sickening knot as she and Alfie watched *Sandpiper II* splinter on the rocks.

'We're idiots!' First the lookout fire, now the raft.

90

These days they couldn't seem to get anything right.

'We won't give in though.'

'What do you mean?'

'We'll build another one.'

He shook his head, and shuddered at the thought of what would have happened if he and Fleur had been on board *Sandpiper II* when it had smashed against the rocks. 'You can if you like. I don't think it's worth it.' What had just happened proved what Alfie had suspected all along – if a raft couldn't even stand up to the ebb and flow of normal tides in shallow water, what chance did they have of building one strong enough to sail all the way down to Misty Island?

'So that's it – we give up? We stay stranded on Dolphin Island for ever?' Fleur turned and walked angrily up the beach.

He ran after her. 'I didn't say that, did I? I'm only saying that a raft isn't the answer.'

She stopped to confront him, sounding desperate. 'What then, Alfie? Go on – tell me how we're ever going to get away from here ...'

'A plane,' he mumbled incoherently. 'A ship.

Someone will find us eventually. Oh, I don't know!'

Shaking her head, she walked on until they reached base camp. 'Where's Mia?' she asked. 'What's she up to now, for goodness' sake?'

'Dunno – probably playing a game inside the shelter.'

'Mia!' Fleur called. When there was no answer, she made a more careful search and spotted prints in the sand from the soles of Mia's new trainers. 'Typical,' she groaned. 'It looks as if she's gone off on her own without telling anyone.'

*

After a slow, halting climb Mia reached Butterfly Falls. The cold mist settled on her skin and made her shiver. Today there were no pretty butterflies dancing in the sunlight or any other sign of life. She began to wonder if she ought to go back down to base camp.

But no – she was more than halfway up the cliff path and she didn't like the idea of leaving Monkey lying on the ledge. She knew exactly where she must have left him: in a niche in the rock, still wearing the pirate's eyepatch that Alfie had made. So Mia gritted her teeth and carried on, following the glow from the lookout fire.

'This way.' Alfie picked up a clear print at the edge of the camp. 'It looks like she's gone up the cliff path.'

'Quick, let's go after her.' Normally Fleur wouldn't have worried too much because Mia was agile and fearless. She'd used the steep path a hundred times. But today was different because of the thick mist. 'We don't want her to get lost.'

They set off through the swirling clouds, carefully picking their way. When they came to a patch of soft earth close to the falls, they discovered another footprint.

'Mia!' Above the splash of water on to rocks, Alfie gave his loudest call.

There was no reply.

*

Mia reached Lookout Point at last and gave a sigh of relief. The sight of the fire reassured her and she walked quickly along the ledge to the spot where she'd left Monkey.

'Monkey?' Her voice fell flat as she looked all around.

He wasn't in the niche after all. Had he fallen out? What had happened to him?

Above her head there was a scrabbling sound and a sudden screeching and chattering. Though she couldn't see them, Mia recognized the sound of macaques fighting between themselves. That must be it; one of the real monkeys had jumped down on to the ledge and grabbed her Monkey and now they were squabbling over him. If she was quick, she could follow them and get him back.

She ran along the ledge and up on to the mountainside. The macaques were still screeching but they'd moved higher up the slope, across the open scrubland towards the jungle. There was more scrabbling and the sound of loose gravel sliding towards her. As she stopped to listen, she felt large, cold drops of rain fall on her face and shoulders.

*

'Mia, where are you?' Fleur and Alfie kept up a constant call as they followed her trail.

'Why doesn't she answer?' Fleur asked as they approached Lookout Point.

'She probably can't hear us.' Alfie was amazed by how much the mist deadened all sounds. The waves breaking on the shore seemed miles away instead of a few hundred metres. He thought he identified the screech of monkeys from further up the mountains but couldn't be sure. 'Do you see any more footprints?'

'Yes – one here. In the soft ground at the edge of the ledge, pointing up the slope.'

Alfie shook his head in disbelief. 'I didn't think even Mia would be this stupid.' *To wander off in the mist without telling anyone, to climb the mountain by herself.*

'This is serious,' Fleur muttered with a quickening heartbeat. 'It's starting to rain. She'll get soaked. Mia, for heaven's sake – where are you?'

Chapter Eight

There was no turning back – Fleur and Alfie had to climb on through the mist and rain. It fell slowly at first, in big, cold drops that splashed on to their bare arms and legs, but it turned quickly into a deluge even worse than the rains that had battered the island during the night. They hunched their shoulders and battled through the downpour, determined to follow in Mia's footsteps.

With the dark, shadowy mass of the jungle just visible through the fog, Alfie stopped. 'It's no good, we've lost her tracks – the rain's washed them away.'

'This is impossible,' Fleur agreed.

'Mia!' Alfie yelled at the top of his voice. The name was carried away by a strong wind that swept down from the mountain top and by the sound of water streaming down the rocky hillside. Rain loosened pebbles that clattered together in their rolling, tumbling slide towards Lookout Point.

Fleur was the first to question their decision to track Mia up the mountainside. 'What if she didn't come this way in the first place?'

'She did – we saw the footprint, remember.'

'But what if she set off and then decided to turn back?'

Alfie closed his eyes to think this through. 'Then we'd have seen her.'

'Not in this fog.'

'OK, so she'd have heard us calling for her.'

'Maybe not – not with the wind blowing so hard and the rain pelting down.' Fleur wasn't sure of anything any more.

'So what do we do?' As Alfie asked the question, he felt the pebbles under his feet shift and he lost his balance. He scrambled back to his feet. 'Do we carry on climbing up or do we go down and find shelter?'

The answer came to them wordlessly on the wind. A strong, wet blast hit them and brought the unmistakable sight of Mia's hat tumbling down the mountainside straight towards them. At the last second, the wind lifted it and sent it whirling out of reach, its red and yellow feathers still securely anchored to the hatband.

Alfie's heart thudded with fresh alarm.

'We carry on,' Fleur muttered. She leaned into the wind and dragged herself up the mountain with Alfie close behind.

On every side, the rain tore up shallow-rooted shrubs. It sent red mud, pebbles and small rocks sliding down the slope, threatening to drag their feet from under them.

'It'll be better to crawl,' she decided as nearby rocks grated slowly along the flooded ground, caught up in a widening stream of mud. 'Careful, Alfie – watch the landslide to our right. There's a clump of trees straight ahead – let's make for that.'

Almost blinded by the downpour, he followed her, having to feel his way with his hands. The rain pelted down on his back, the sight of Mia's hat bowled along by the mighty wind staying with him as he crawled on. He hoped and prayed that she'd found shelter in time.

'Once we reach the jackfruit trees, I think we should stop for a while,' Fleur called over her shoulder, though she could barely make out the familiar tall, smooth trunks less than ten metres ahead.

It was easier said than done. The unstoppable river of sludge grew wider and deeper, sweeping everything in its path – small boulders and tree branches torn off by the hurricane-force wind, palm tree fronds and thick lianas, whole shrubs uprooted and slithering down the mountainside.

'Just a few more metres,' Fleur promised him.

He gasped for breath. There was dark red mud everywhere – covering his limbs and face. It was in his hair and up his nostrils.

'Here. Give me your hand.' She'd reached the trees and solid ground. 'Alfie, this way!'

A sliding rock slammed against his arm, knocking him sideways. He rolled on to his back and felt himself carried away by the mud then he managed to roll on to his belly and clutch at a prickly shrub that tore loose in his grasp. Finally his foot lodged against a solid boulder and he used this to propel himself forward, back up the slope, clawing his way towards Fleur.

'Grab my hand,' she hissed again, her heart thumping against her ribs.

He closed his fingers around her wrist and felt her haul him up the slope. 'Thanks.' He coughed and spat out mud as he flopped down next to her.

'Oh, Alfie!' Instead of being relieved that he was safe, she gave a desperate shake of her head. 'Look what I found.' She clasped an object in her right hand that she seemed afraid to show him.

'What is it?' He cowered under the jackfruit tree, blinded by rain, mist and mud.

Fleur held out her hand. Resting in her palm was a shiny object hanging from a piece of frayed blue string. 'It's Mia's dolphin charm,' she said with a catch in her voice.

He took it from her and examined it with trembling fingers. 'Where did you find it?'

She let out a low sob. 'Snagged on this myrtle bush. It means she made it this far before the mudslide started. Oh, Alfie!'

With a sharp intake of breath, he closed his fingers over Mia's lucky charm. 'I know,' he whispered as he stared into the jungle behind them and felt the full force of what Fleur had said. 'I know!'

*

A deep rumble sounded across Dolphin Island, from north to south and from east to west – the noise of rocks and boulders carried along by waist-high rivers of mud that ran down the burned, bare mountainside. Two centimetres of rain fell in fifteen minutes on to ash-coated ground already laid waste by wildfire. The unstoppable mudslide carried everything in its path – it tore at roots and toppled whole trees, shifted boulders which smashed through scrubland, destroying the habitats of macaques, cassowaries, rats and wild boar. Birds of paradise and cockatoos flew clear of the rain-lashed trees while sandpipers, herons and other shore birds sought shelter in caves until the storm had passed and the river of mud had come to rest.

Then, as if the island had not suffered enough, high tide and driving winds brought enormous waves crashing on to the shore, smashing on to headlands and flinging jetsam on to white beaches, littering them with ugly debris made up of palm tree trunks, sheets of metal, mounds of plastic, rubber and all the discarded rubbish of the modern world that lay far across the blue ocean.

Rain, wind and tide wreaked havoc. It seemed as if the Fishers' beautiful paradise island would never be the same again.

*

Alfie held Mia's charm in the palm of his hand. The wind stripped the leaves off the jackfruit trees and sent fruit hurtling to the ground. Rain pelted down on his head and dug deep muddy channels through the bare slope at their feet.

Fleur put her hands to her ears to block out the rumble of mud sliding down past Lookout Point over the edge of the cliff on to Butterfly Falls and beyond that to the beach below. From high on the mountain she heard boulders crash down. *Make it end!* she prayed silently. *Let Mia and Mum and Dad be safe!*

Mum and Dad! Fleur pictured them seeking shelter in Mangrove Bay and prayed that they would be out of harm's way.

The rain kept on falling and the wind howling until at last the mist started to clear. Then low cloud slowly lifted from the dark mountain peak, revealing newly felled trees in the jungle behind them. Giant trunks had toppled to expose tangles of roots torn clear of the ground. Down the slope from where they'd taken refuge, more boulders came to rest by Lookout Point, teetering on the edge of the cliff.

Fleur held out her hand to test the rainfall. 'It's easing off,' she said. 'And the wind's dying down.'

When Alfie glanced at her face, he hardly recognized her. Her eyes were enormous and dark, her mouth pinched and puckered in an expression of deep dread. 'So what?' he whispered back.

'We have to start looking for Mia again.'

He frowned and tried to get his bearings. The storm seemed to have changed everything – there were none of the usual landmarks to go by. 'Do we even know where we are?'

'Yes – there's Lookout Point. And these are the trees where we usually come to collect fruit and wood.' Fleur took a closer look at their surroundings and felt a fresh jolt of fear run through her body as she identified the place where they'd come across the giant reptile eggs. The heap of twigs and leaves was gone, of course, and there was a thick layer of mud over everything, but she recognized the spot by the hollow in the ground. She took a deep breath then cupped her hands to her mouth to call out Mia's name.

'Mia!' Now that the fog had lifted, the sound carried further. 'Mia – it's Fleur and Alfie. Where are you?'

*

The rain stopped and the clouds slowly parted to reveal a pale yellow sun. Steam began to rise from the soaked earth.

Deep in the jungle, skinks and rats crept out of hiding and tree frogs began to croak.

Mia did not dare to move. She stayed hidden by creepers, crouching behind an overhanging rock where she'd taken refuge while branches crashed down and the storm destroyed everything around. *Don't move. Don't breathe. Don't cry. Close eyes – don't look.*

But gradually things had started to stir around her. A bedraggled tree kangaroo crept warily down a nearby

104

tree trunk, head first, with its long, thick tail trailing behind. It sniffed at the figure huddled close to the rock, gave it a wide berth then carried on. A family of macaques followed more nimbly, straight down the same trunk and on along a fallen log towards the sunlight, swinging through vines and showering more water on to the already sodden earth.

Open eyes – find out what that was. Monkeys. OK, close again. Wait. Don't move.

Mia heard a creature give a loud snort. It sounded like a pig. She knew there were wild boar in the jungle. They had sharp tusks. If she kept very still the boar would pass by without noticing her.

Why had she come here by herself? She hadn't even found Monkey and then it had started to rain so hard that she'd had to run under the trees, but she hadn't been able to see where she was going in the fog and she'd stumbled the wrong way – further into the jungle instead of staying on the edge. She'd got caught up in bushes and tripped over tree roots and lianas, got even more lost than before. Branches had broken off trees and crashed down to the ground. Big palm fronds had fallen, just missing her head. She'd hidden by a rock and waited for the storm to end.

Now steam rose from the slimy, dark brown mud on the jungle floor. *Open eyes, take a look.* Birds hopped along branches – black and white, white and yellow, green ones that squawked. *Which way did the monkeys go?*

From deeper in the shadows Mia heard more movement. She cowered against the rock as two macaques broke through the bushes and passed close by without seeing her. *Only monkeys again – phew!* Then there was a low hissing sound. *What hisses in the jungle? Is it a snake?* Mia, who had been slowly gaining courage, pressed back against her wet rock.

There was another, louder hiss. The thing was coming closer. She could hear it breaking twigs and swishing through leaves. A hiss, then a rumble, then heavy footsteps – she opened her eyes in terror.

It stalked towards her, swinging its great, flat head from side to side, approaching slowly on its bandy legs, flicking out its forked tongue – the stealthy, hissing Creature of her nightmares, with long claws and a body

106

covered in scales, like a huge dragon. Here it came, hungrily hunting her, opening its jaws to reveal two rows of blood-covered teeth.

Fixed to the spot in terror as the Creature advanced, Mia opened her mouth and screamed.

*

Alfie and Fleur heard a high, fearful human cry. They reacted instantly by following the chilling sound into the steaming jungle, leaping over tree trunks and grasping at lianas to steady them on their way.

'We're coming, Mia!' Fleur shouted as she pushed aside thick green foliage, ducked under low branches, almost lost her balance then recovered and scrambled on.

There was a second scream.

The huge, reddish-green Creature stopped in its tracks. Its mouth gaped open and its tongue flicked towards Mia as it swished its long, thick tail.

A dragon, a horrible dragon with a flat head and tiny eyes, legs as thick as tree trunks, sharp claws, pointed teeth – everything that she dreaded!

'Mia, where are you?' Alfie used low branches to

swing ahead of Fleur as he jumped from one flat rock
to the next. There wasn't much daylight – just
dappled sun in small patches, and white steam rising
from the mud.

'Alfie, Fleur – help me!' Mia cried.

'Hold on – we're coming!' Fleur caught up with Alfie
and they followed the direction of Mia's voice.

The dragon swung its heavy head as it advanced
again. It took its time, lifting its scaly legs and planting

its clawed feet on tree roots and fallen branches, cracking them with its great weight.

'Help me!' Mia's cry pierced the jungle.

Fleur and Alfie found her hunched down behind a rock. When the creature saw them, it opened its jaws wide and raised itself high on to its hind legs so that it was more than two metres tall and towering over Mia's rock. It hissed and swiped its front claws in their direction, warning them off.

They took in the scene and froze. Fleur knew that if they made a false move the Komodo dragon would move in swiftly for the kill.

Because Fleur had finally worked it out – the Creature was a Komodo dragon, the same one that had terrified Mia once before and had laid her giant eggs in the carefully concealed nest at the jungle's edge. A Komodo, the largest lizard in the world – swift runner and stealthy daytime hunter, meat-eater that reared up to lash out with her feet and knock over her helpless victim before she moved in and swallowed her prey whole.

Chapter Nine

Steam rose around the giant lizard as she raised one clawed back leg from the ground, ready to kick out. Above her head, a group of monkeys swung through the vines, screeching and fleeing from the monster below.

Fleur gathered a sobbing Mia into her arms. Alfie stood defiant guard over them, legs wide apart, head tilted back to meet the monster's gaze.

For a few seconds the mob of monkeys drew the Komodo's attention away from Mia, Fleur and Alfie. She let out another rumbling hiss and swiped her front claws at the macaques, displaying two rows of razor-sharp teeth. Then she came down heavily and lurched sideways into the mud before heaving herself out on to a fallen trunk close to Mia's rock. She got ready to raise herself up on to her hind legs for a second time and resume her attack.

Mia hid her face against Fleur's shoulder. Alfie stood firm.

The monkeys screamed, tugging at the loops of thick lianas until their combined weight brought the long vines down over their maddened enemy. The creepers landed across her back then caught around her limbs and claws, giving Fleur, Mia and Alfie vital extra moments. From the safety of a thick branch the macaques stamped their feet in a triumphant dance.

'Run!' Alfie gasped as the Creature struggled to emerge from the tangle of lianas.

Fleur pulled Mia to her feet and kept hold of her hand. 'Don't let go!' she warned as they all scrambled on to the log. Ahead was a gleam of sunlight, behind them blackness and terror.

The monkeys stamped and screamed. The storm-weakened branch bent under their weight. There was an almighty crack as it split from the trunk and the macaques leaped clear. It crashed to the ground, striking the lizard's head as it fell. She toppled back into the deep slime.

'Quick – run!' It was Alfie's voice this time.

Still holding Mia's hand, Fleur led the way towards sunlight and safety.

As the macaques swung to the ground to taunt their enemy, the Komodo sank further into the mud. She clawed at the fallen branch but only succeeded in dragging it down with her.

Alfie glanced round. 'Keep going!' he cried. For once the inhospitable jungle and marauding monkeys had proved to be their friends. 'The dragon's stuck – it can't get out of the mud. We can make it if we're quick.'

To the sound of screeching monkeys and the suck of mud as the Komodo fought to free herself, Fleur, Mia and Alfie clambered breathlessly from the log on to a flat rock and then on to another log, forging a way through the dense forest towards the light.

*

Even when they reached the edge of the jungle they didn't dare to look back. As they emerged into the strengthening sunlight, they sucked air into their lungs and kept on running down the mountain, fleeing the nightmare that they'd just escaped.

They were greeted by a scene of destruction. Swathes of steaming red mud coated the scrubland between them and Lookout Point. Boulders and tree branches lay strewn across the hillside.

'What's happened to our poor island?' Mia cried. She tugged desperately at Fleur's hand.

'Don't stop.' Fleur drew her on down the slope, taking care to avoid areas of wet mud glistening in the sunlight. 'Rain is what happened, Mi-mi. Rain and wind and mud.'

'Do we know where Mum and Dad are?' Mia stared down the hillside then out towards the ocean and the misty grey horizon.

'Not exactly. They headed off to Mangrove Bay, remember?'

Mia shook her head.

'Thank goodness they weren't around,' Fleur muttered. 'If they'd been tending the fire at Lookout Point, they might have been caught in the mudslide and swept over the cliff.'

'But where are they?'

'Try not to worry. I'm sure they found somewhere

114

safe to shelter until the rain stopped.' Drawing close to Lookout Point, Fleur saw that a pile of boulders blocked their way on to the ledge. She took one quick glance up at the jungle to make sure that the Komodo hadn't followed them. 'It's OK to rest for a minute,' she decided.

But Alfie was already thinking ahead. He climbed on to the nearest boulder then looked down towards Butterfly Falls. His stomach churned as he saw the damage that the mudslide had done to the narrow cliff path. In fact, the old way was impassable due to fallen rocks and slimy mud. 'We'll have to find a new way down,' he declared – a skinny, lonely figure standing on the brink of destruction. His orange T-shirt and red shorts were caked with mud, his hair plastered to his head.

'How come?' Fleur came to join him. 'Oh, I see.' She stared in dismay at what was left of the path. 'Couldn't we try to clear the rocks away?'

'No. They'd be too heavy.' He picked out a shorter, narrower ledge to their right that was clear. 'We have to go that way – the sooner the better.'

His words made Mia and Fleur glance back up the

hill. It still seemed possible that the Komodo might pull herself out of the swamp, emerge from the jungle and pursue them down the mountain.

'Let's get a move on then.' This time Fleur let Alfie take the lead.

He picked his way, carefully testing out the ground before he put his full weight on to the muddy surface. 'It's slippery just here,' he warned. 'Mind your head on this overhang. Cool – there's a clear patch of gravel ahead. And I reckon that from there I can work out a safe way down to the beach.'

Relieved that he'd taken charge of the route, Fleur supervised Mia. 'Careful.' She steadied her as she hastily followed Alfie without minding where she put her feet. 'Don't go too close to the edge.'

It seemed to take for ever but at last they made it to the new vantage point, able to make out Butterfly Falls to their left and Base Camp Bay directly below. A rocky overhang hid their shelter from view.

'We can't see a whole lot,' Alfie admitted with a frown. 'But we know one thing for sure – our fire at base camp has gone out as well as the one at Lookout Point.'

True, there was no smoke. It was a bad blow – without fire they wouldn't be able to cook or to send a signal to planes and ships. 'No problem – we'll light another as soon as we get down there.' Fleur refused to feel scared or defeated. 'Lead the way, Alfie.'

They set off again, forced to take a zigzag route to stay clear of the mudslide. But at least the air felt fresher and the sea was clear azure, with darker blue patches marking out the shapes of underwater coral reefs, its surface sparkling in the sun. Gentle waves broke on the shore. For a while it was possible to imagine that, apart from the fire, they would find base camp exactly the same as when they'd left it.

They reached the bottom of the cliff and jumped on to the sand then ran towards the group of palm trees that protected their shelter from the wind. It was only when Fleur glimpsed the treetops above a rocky ridge that she sensed that something was different. *One – two – three – four* ... She stopped counting. There should have been six trees. Without saying a word, she ran ahead until base camp came into view. The mudslide had left four palm trees standing. Two others had been uprooted and fallen across their shelter, smashing through the roof and demolishing the walls. Then mud and boulders had poured down from Butterfly Falls, wrecking what was left of their camp.

Alfie and Mia caught up with Fleur. All three stood in stunned silence.

The roof of their shelter had caved in. Red mud had oozed over the platform and boulders had knocked away two of the stilts, tilting the whole thing at an angle of forty-five degrees. The mud had spread out in an ugly dark stain across the white beach, swamping their fire and reaching beyond their food store and stack of firewood before coming to a halt just short of George's Cave.

Fleur and Alfie shook their heads in disbelief. Their beautiful home stood in ruins. Everything they'd built in order to survive on Dolphin Island was smashed or else submerged under a layer of sticky brown mud that steamed and dried rapidly in the midday heat.

Mia gave a cry and ran forward. She stumbled in the soft sand then picked herself up and ran again, only stopping outside the entrance to George's Cave where she broke down and started to cry.

Fleur followed slowly. Their place of safety was gone – their beds, their map, every pot, every pan lost under a thick layer of brown sludge. As she trudged across the sand, her insides felt hollow, carved out by a sharp sense of despair. And what about George? Had he managed to escape the terrible, gut-wrenching mudslide?

Alfie didn't move. He tried to take in what had happened, picturing the moment when the mighty mudslide had reached the edge of the cliff then spilled over on to their camp. There would have been a roar and the sound of boulders smashing on to the roof, a rush of mud. All their possessions destroyed in a matter of seconds. He took one slow step forward then stopped. *I can't go any nearer*. He glanced at Fleur with her arms around Mia by George's Cave then turned and walked away.

*

'Come inside the cave, out of the sun.' Fleur spoke gently to Mia.

'What are we going to do now?' Mia sobbed.

Fleur cleared debris from the cave entrance. She saw that the high tide had flooded the normally dry interior and left behind a heap of shells, driftwood and the usual man-made rubbish. There was a strong smell of salt water and rotting seaweed. 'Come inside,' she said again as she took hold of Mia's hand.

Mia pulled away. 'Fleur, I don't like it.'

'I know. Neither do I.'

'Where's Alfie going?'

'I'm not sure.'

'Where are Mum and Dad?'

'Mi-mi, I wish I knew. What we have to do is wait here and give them time to make their way back.' Doubt gnawed at her, but she chose to hide her fears.

From inside the cave Fleur looked out at the sea – the only thing that the storm hadn't altered. Waves still broke against *Merlin's* reef. They rolled serenely into the bay. Somewhere out there, Jazz, Stormy and Pearl swam with their pod. 'But I'll tell you what – why don't we sit here for a few minutes to get our breaths back then go and see what we can rescue from the shelter?'

'OK.' Reluctantly Mia entered the cave. She held her nose and picked her way through the seaweed and rubbish then sat on a ledge next to Fleur. 'Can we mend the roof of our shelter?'

A smile flitted across Fleur's face. If only it were that easy. 'We can try,' she replied wearily.

'And build a fire?' Mia quickly forgot about the bad smell. She turned to Fleur with another eager suggestion.

'Yes, if we can find the lens to start it with.'

'And have something to eat?' Realizing that she was hungry, Mia jumped down from the ledge.

'We can definitely do that,' Fleur agreed. She picked up a wet palm frond cast up by the waves and broke it in half. 'Here, Mi-mi – use this as a parasol.'

'Hey!' Mia took the palm frond and walked out into the sun then gave a cry of surprise, because, stashed away in a niche in the rock, was Monkey. She took him down and shook sand from him. He was damp and minus his pirate eyepatch but otherwise none the worse for wear. 'This is where I left you!'

'After all that!' Fleur didn't have enough energy to feel annoyed. Instead, she watched Mia clutch her soft toy and chat to him as she ran up the beach.

'Look at me, Monkey – I've got mud all over my lovely new T-shirt. And we saw a dragon in the jungle – a real live one. Wait till I tell Mum and Dad.'

With a deep sigh, Fleur followed. She saw Alfie in the distance, perched on a rock on the headland, staring out to sea. She waved and after a while he waved back.

Mia stopped to wait for Fleur at the edge of the mudslide.

'First, the food store.' Fleur decided on their plan of action then tested out the mud. Her foot broke through the sun-baked crust to reveal a thin layer of sludge. 'This will soon soak away into the sand,' she decided. 'Come on, Mi-mi; we can go ahead.'

Watched by two white herons flying low overhead, they headed for the crevice in the rock where they stored their food. Fleur cleared away a covering of mud then lifted the stone lid to find that the contents were clean and dry. She took out half a coconut.

Smelling dried fish inside the fissure, the herons swooped down.

'Shoo!' Mia sent them away with a whoosh of her

palm frond while Fleur pushed the lid back into place. 'How do we get the coconut out of the shell?'

'We'll have to break it into smaller pieces then gnaw it out with our front teeth.' Fleur smashed the shell as she spoke.

'Like monkeys?'

'Exactly. Here you are.' Now that she knew there was no danger of them starving, she could afford to relax a little. In spite of her worries about Katie and James, the horrible hollow feeling began to recede.

Mia chewed and sucked at the piece of coconut. 'Now what?'

'Next thing, Able Seaman Mia, we board the wreck.'

'Aye-aye, Captain!' She saluted then marched towards the ruined shelter to await the next order.

'Keep watch,' Fleur told her. 'Cutlass at the ready.'

Mia held her palm frond aloft. 'Cutlass at the ready, Captain!'

Fleur stepped on to the lowest end of the sloping platform. Then she crept under one of the fallen tree trunks and began to clear a way into the interior of the shelter. She scooped away mud and stones until her hand came into contact with a large square object. 'I've found a bed,' she reported back to Mia.

'Yay!' Mia grinned then waved at Alfie who was walking swiftly across the beach. 'Fleur found a bed!'

Within seconds he'd climbed on to the platform and joined Fleur to help her lift the bed out. 'Sorry about earlier,' he muttered. 'I just needed to sit by myself for a bit.'

'It was a nasty shock,' she agreed. 'But at least this bed isn't broken.'

Together they shoved it to the edge of the platform. 'Stand clear, Mia,' Alfie warned before they lowered it on to the beach.

'Aye-aye, Captain. Can I come up now?'

'No, it's too cramped up here. Carry on standing guard for us – you're doing a great job.' Fleur cleared mud away from a second bed frame then uncovered the red plastic box containing their first-aid kit resting on top of it. Inside there were scissors and bandages, plus some headache pills, antiseptic cream and sticking plasters. It was also where Katie stored their precious lens. 'Cool! Give this to Mia,' she told Alfie.

He ducked under the tree trunk and handed over the box then went back to tug at the second bed. 'Maybe we'll be able to rebuild the shelter after Mum and Dad get back and we've cleared all the mud away.'

Fleur grimaced as she looked up through the massive hole in the roof then around at the claggy, brown mud slathered over everything. 'You're kidding.'

'OK, it's too badly damaged.' He admitted they'd have to build a complete new shelter. 'But look at this.' He spotted a speck of yellow and pulled out one of the life-jackets from *Merlin*. 'It'll be fine; it just needs a wash.'

'And this.' Fleur unhooked a square of crumpled canvas from one of the wall panels. It was their map of Dolphin Island but the rain and mud had erased all trace of the original drawing. 'Oh, well ...'

They toiled on, kneeling on the sloping platform and scrabbling elbow-deep in mud to salvage everything they could – clam shell plates and coconut shell bowls plus Alfie's knife, lengths of rope and the hammock that James slept in. By the end of the afternoon they'd carried everything down to the shoreline, washed it in the sea then made a neat pile by the entrance to George's Cave. As Fleur and Alfie stood back to admire their salvage work, a sudden thought struck Mia and she ran back up the beach. She went down on her belly and wriggled under the platform, found what she was looking for then sprinted back, straight past them to the water's edge.

'The conch!' she declared as she rinsed it clean. She held her dripping find high in the air.

Alfie took it from her. 'It's in perfect condition – not a mark on it,' he said after close inspection. Then, as if suddenly remembering something, he put his hand into his pocket. 'Here's your lucky charm,' he told Mia. 'We found it on the mountain.'

Her face lit up with delight and she asked Fleur to tie the shiny mother-of-pearl dolphin around her neck before climbing on to her favourite ledge close to the entrance to the cave. 'Now all we have to do is carry on waiting for Mum and Dad to arrive!'

Chapter Ten

'No time to sit around.' Fleur decided that there was more work to be done. 'We can't sleep in the shelter any more so we'll have to clear the rubbish out of George's Cave and put the beds and the hammock in there for the night.'

Alfie knew that this made sense so he set about dragging seaweed from inside the cave. 'This stuff stinks,' he complained when he dumped it at the water's edge. As he went back inside for more, he asked Mia to lend a hand.

She shook her head. 'I'm waiting for Mum and Dad.'

'Why can't you do both?'

"Cos I can't.' Still perched on her ledge, she stared doggedly at the headland separating them from Turtle Beach.

'Let's leave her.' Fleur understood why Mia looked and sounded worried. 'It is weird,' she confessed in a whisper as she and Alfie carried another load of debris out of the cave. 'I expected Mum and Dad to be back by now.'

'Me too.' He picked a couple of useful clam shells out of the pile. 'So why aren't they?'

'I haven't a clue. I guess it depends where they were when the storm broke. If they were all the way down in Mangrove Bay like they planned, it would take them most of the afternoon to make their way home.'

'That's true.' Alfie didn't sound convinced. 'You don't suppose something bad happened to them during the storm?'

'Like what?' Fleur didn't want to consider this so she shrugged it off then hurried back to the cave. 'Mia, help me drag this bed inside.'

Like an accident. He realized it was better to keep this thought to himself. *A rockfall, for instance. Or a flood or a mudslide somewhere else on the island.* There was a long list of disasters that might have held James and Katie up.

'Do I have to help?' Mia frowned at Fleur.

'Yes – please!' The sun was already sinking and it would soon be dark. Fleur looked long and hard at her little sister's sulky face. 'Oh, never mind – I can manage.'

Mia stayed where she was. 'I don't want to sleep in George's Cave,' she announced as Alfie carried the hammock inside. 'What if the dragon comes and gets us?'

'It won't,' he promised. 'Anyway, it wasn't really a dragon.'

'Fleur said it was. A kimono dragon – that's what she called it.'

'Not kimono; Komodo.' He stopped what he was doing. 'Listen, Mi-mi – it was a big, big lizard, not a dragon. Dragons that breathe fire aren't real. And the Komodo lives in the jungle. It won't come down to the beach.'

'It might.' Mia's voice quavered.

'It hasn't so far and we've been here eight weeks and two days.'

From inside the cave, Fleur overheard Alfie's explanation. From what she'd read and seen on videos she knew that the giant lizards did prefer a tropical forest habitat. But they were also known to hunt in open grassland and they had a large home range of around two square kilometres. What's more, they could run fast – up to thirteen miles per hour. They would stalk and corner their prey then kick out and smash it to the ground. Then they would tear it apart with their claws and teeth. And Komodo dragons weren't fussy about what they ate – geckos, goats, wild boar, other Komodos. They had even been known to kill humans.

'We'll be safe in the cave,' Alfie reassured Mia.

'You know what?' Fleur came out with a brisk, no-nonsense air. 'Why don't we block the entrance to the cave, just in case? The fence panel that we found the other day is still in the wood pile – we could use that.'

Alfie nodded. 'How about it, Mi-mi?'

Mia sniffed then grudgingly agreed.

'We'll have to be quick though.' With luck, there was still enough daylight to do the job. 'You stay here, Mia, and keep watch like you said.'

As Fleur and Alfie ran back to base camp and waded

through the thick, gloopy mud, they planned ahead.

'This fence panel is pretty flimsy,' Alfie realized as they pulled it clear. 'The Komodo could smash straight through it.'

'But you were the one who said it hasn't left the jungle,' Fleur reminded him.

'So we're only blocking the entrance to make Mia feel happier – yeah?' There was a wobble in his voice nevertheless.

'I guess.' If that was what Alfie wanted to think, then let him. But Fleur wasn't so sure. After all, what if the bloodthirsty Komodo did follow them as far as the beach? Shaking off the thought, she took a quick look around the ruins of what had been their home. 'We could still make a stronger barrier though. Where did you leave that roll of barbed wire?'

'Over there.' In the fading light he waded through more sludge and pulled the wire out from a crevice in the rock close to the food store. 'Good thinking – we can reinforce the fence panel with this.'

Eager to build up their barricade before the sun sank, they hurried back to George's Cave where Alfie slung the hammock between two rocks then dragged the second bed inside. Meanwhile Fleur worked out a way of propping the fence against the entrance. 'We'll be able to fix it in place with piles of stones.'

From her ledge, Mia watched Alfie uncoil the barbed wire and stretch it out across the entrance. 'What if Mum and Dad come back while we're asleep? How will they get in?'

'Don't worry – it'll be fine.'

'But how will they?'

'I said, it'll be fine.' There was no satisfying Mia when she was in this mood. 'Come inside,' Alfie told her. 'It's time to go to sleep.'

The sun, a ball of red fire, slipped out of sight behind the mountain and darkness fell. The barrier was in place.

But inside the cave, Alfie, Mia and Fleur were wide awake in the hammock and on the wooden beds.

'This isn't good,' Alfie whispered into the dark, still air. 'Mum and Dad ought to have been back ages ago. We should have set out to look for them.'

'How could we?' Fleur challenged. 'We could

easily have missed them. Then they'd have arrived at base camp and found it deserted. They'd have thought the worst. Anyway, it soon got too dark to go out and search.'

In the pitch-black night, every creak and scratch, every gust of wind that whisked the barbed wire against the wooden fence panel made them jump out of their skins. The sound of pebbles grating on the ebbing tide reminded Fleur and Alfie of the terrifying mudslide on the mountain, and to Mia, the endless rush of waves on the shore was the deep hiss and roar of the monster as it emerged from the jungle.

*

Daylight crept into the cave but no one moved.

James and Katie had not returned.

'Fleur?' Mia's high voice broke the thick silence. 'Is it time to get up?'

Fleur woke up from a shallow sleep and rubbed her eyes. There was just enough light to see Mia sitting at the edge of her bed and Alfie standing by the entrance as if he'd spent the whole night there keeping watch. It took her a few seconds to remember where she was.

Then memories of the previous day flooded in.

'Wait here while I take a look outside.' Alfie removed the fence panel and the barbed-wire barricade. He stepped out cautiously and surveyed his surroundings – two dark, empty headlands, a smooth white beach and their base camp submerged under a tide of mud. There was no sign of the Komodo, thank goodness. 'Sun's up,' he told them in a flat voice.

Mia carried Monkey out of the cave on to the beach while Fleur took her time to come round. As she stared up at the roof of the cave, she felt a heavy weight pressing down on her chest. Her mouth was dry and her head felt as if it was stuffed with cotton wool.

'What day is it?' Mia asked Alfie as they wandered down to the water's edge.

'Day 59. It's a Wednesday.' *Never forget what day it is.* This had been Alfie's mantra ever since they'd been washed up on the beach. If he lost track of the days it would be a sign that he'd given up hope of ever being rescued.

Fleur overheard their conversation and sat up slowly. *Day 59 – chores to be done. Water, food, fire.* She forced herself to set about the daily routine. *Mum and Dad, what on earth's happened to you?* she thought.

From a shallow ledge close to the roof of the cave George gazed down at Fleur with his unblinking stare.

How will we get up to Butterfly Falls? she wondered wearily. *The mudslide wrecked the cliff path. OK, so we'll have to go the long way round. We've probably got enough food to last for a day or two. But what about the fires?*

George shifted from his ledge. He clung to the rough wall with his sticky toe pads and made his way slowly down to the ground.

'Mum and Dad didn't come.' Mia stood forlornly at the shoreline, staring out at the reef.

'No,' Alfie agreed quietly. Wednesday, Day 59. Following on from Tuesday, Day 58, the day of catastrophe when everything on Dolphin Island had changed forever. 'Not yet.'

Why not? he asked himself. *Has one of them been hurt? The minute it gets properly light, I'm going to set off for Mangrove Bay and find out!*

Fleur forced herself to stand up. The weight around

her chest hadn't shifted. *What's wrong with me?*

Her little pet gecko cocked his head to one side and whisked his tail.

I hardly slept – that's what's wrong. No, that's not it. What then? She stumbled to the entrance without noticing George and saw Mia and Alfie standing like mud-caked statues, staring out to sea. *Mum and Dad aren't back.* The crushing realization hit Fleur hard. *Now I'm the one who has to take charge.*

*

The sun rose above the horizon and Fleur walked up to Alfie and Mia. 'We need water,' she reminded them. 'We'll have to go back to the shelter and dig out some plastic bottles. I don't want us to split up today. We should all go up to Butterfly Falls together.'

'No – I want to look for Mum and Dad.' Instead of skipping up the beach as usual, Mia stayed rooted to the spot.

'She's got a point,' Alfie said to Fleur. 'In fact, I was thinking the same thing. We ought to find them before we do anything else.'

'But we won't get through the day without water.'

The important thing was to keep a clear head and do what Katie and James would have told her to do. 'After we've filled the containers, that's when we can start looking.'

Mia wasn't happy but Alfie reluctantly agreed with Fleur and so they set about rescuing some big water bottles from the ruined shelter then made their slow, hazardous way up the cliff. No one spoke as they picked their way up through mud and fallen rocks to the falls where they drank plenty of cool, refreshing water, filled their bottles then carried them back down to Base Camp Bay.

'Now can we look for Mum and Dad?' Mia clamoured.

Fleur was on tenterhooks as she walked down to the shore and scanned the coastline. She knew one thing for sure: Katie and James had set off for Mangrove Bay well before the monsoon rains had hit the island. The rest remained a mystery – what had happened to stop them hurrying back to base camp, and how had they survived the night? No answers came as she continued to stare out to sea.

'Which way?' Mia wanted to know.

Fleur gave a heavy sigh. 'To Turtle Beach, then on from there until we find them,' she decided. 'Ready, Alfie?'

'Wait a sec.' He stood next to her at the water's edge. Were his eyes playing tricks or had he just seen dolphins swimming along the horizon? He couldn't be sure.

Mia paddled deeper into the water. 'What are you looking at?'

He narrowed his eyes and kept on searching for more dolphin activity. Sure enough, he pinpointed a disturbance in the water and if he looked even more closely he could see a whole pod of twenty or thirty leaping clear of the water and swimming at speed from south to north. 'Look out there!' he gasped.

Fleur and Mia followed the direction of his pointing finger.

'Dolphins,' Fleur murmured. She gave a long sigh of relief, while Mia ran to the cave and brought back the conch shell.

'Quickly – blow it,' she told Alfie. 'Stormy, Pearl and Jazz will help us to find Mum and Dad.'

'Hang on, Mia; we don't know if it's our pod,' Fleur

warned. The Torres Strait was teeming with bottle-nose dolphins, all busily swimming after the plentiful shoals of fish in the deep ocean.

'But it's worth a try.' Alfie raised the conch to his lips and blew a clear, strong note.

The pod of dolphins kept a steady course.

'Maybe they're too far away to hear.' Alfie turned questioningly towards Fleur.

'Try a really high note – that's what they hear best.'

So he blew again and this time they saw three dolphins split off from the pod and swim rapidly towards the island. They cut through the calm water at great speed, leaping high then diving deep underwater, only coming up for air when they drew near the reef.

With a loud cheer Mia threw herself into the water and swam to meet Stormy, who spotted her and gave his shrill whistle. Fleur and Alfie followed and soon they were reunited with Jazz and Pearl. Jazz swam close to Fleur, creaking and clicking out a greeting while Alfie threw one arm around Pearl and rested his head against her side. She joined the dolphin chorus with a series of whistles and chirps.

'Are we glad to see you!' Alfie patted and stroked Pearl, who seemed to smile back at him. She nudged him sideways and turned her head as if inviting him to climb on to her back.

Stormy swam full circle around Mia then came up close and waited patiently as if he knew that this was not a time for games.

Fleur had already climbed astride Jazz. She grasped his dorsal fin and waited for the others to follow her lead. 'All aboard?' she checked.

Within seconds all three were riding their dolphins across Base Camp Bay, feeling the strong, muscular movement of their torpedo-shaped bodies beneath them and enjoying the cold spray as the dolphins smacked their tail flukes against the water. Then Pearl raised her head high above the surface and clapped her jaws together as if asking Alfie what he wanted her to do next.

'Head south.' He patted her side firmly then leaned forward in the direction they wanted to go. 'Keep your eyes peeled,' he yelled at the others as together they rounded the headland to Turtle Beach.

The sight that met them made their hearts sink. Mud had poured down from the mountain and boulders had smashed on to the beach, smothering the area at the base of the cliffs where the stand of bamboos had grown. Trees were down. There was no sign of life – no footprints in the sand, no bird-life, no monkeys.

Fleur shook her head in dismay. 'Let's carry on,' she muttered to Alfie. Perhaps the storm had spared the next beach and they would find their mum and dad there.

So Jazz, Pearl and Stormy swam on, a hundred metres out from the shore, following every curve of the coastline, investigating every inlet until they came to Pirate Cave Beach where the wind had brought down most of the trees.

'At least the mud didn't reach this far,' Alfie remarked. In fact, the beach was as white and inviting as ever. He decided it was worth taking a closer look. 'Wait here,' he told Mia and Fleur then slid from Pearl's back and swam for the shore. He soon reached dry land and called out in a loud voice, 'Mum, Dad – are you there?'

There was no reply.

'Mum, Dad!'

Still no answer, so he ran up the beach to the cave entrance. This seemed the logical place to take shelter during a storm until he remembered that only Mia was small enough to wriggle through the narrow entrance. He knelt down and gave one final shout into the cave to make sure. 'Is anybody there?'

There – there – there?

'Mum, Dad!'

Dad – ad – ad!

No luck. So Alfie sprinted down to the sea and within seconds sat astride Pearl again. 'Nope,' he reported abruptly.

So on they went under the blue sky. The sun was hot on their backs as Pearl, Stormy and Jazz swam close to the shore, steering around jagged reefs and slowing down as they entered shallow water until finally they arrived in the spectacular rocky inlet of Black Crab Cove.

Chapter Eleven

Pearl, Stormy and Jazz carried Alfie, Mia and Fleur into the cove and under the soaring rock arch that marked the beginning of Mangrove Bay – the wide, swampy area to the south where Alfie had cared for Pearl after the shark attack. Then the dolphins turned to head out into deeper water for a long-distance view of the shore.

Alfie gave a shudder as he recognized the dark swamp. A tangled mass of mangrove roots rose clear of the murky water and their branches formed a thick canopy that cut out all daylight. 'I hope we don't have to go in there to search for Mum and Dad,' he muttered to Fleur, who had focused on Black Crab Cove.

She studied the inlet and the black cliffs rising vertically to a height of thirty metres. Then she lowered her gaze to take in the upturned wreck of *Dolphin*. She saw that the wind had whipped the sand dunes high up against her bleached wooden hull and blown down three tall palm trees. Two of the trees had crashed on to the beach and the third had come down directly on to the wreck, smashing a big hole in its ancient side.

'You two stay here – it's my turn to search,' she said quietly. She let go of Jazz's fin and slipped into the water, surprised to find him swimming beside her until he almost grounded himself on the white sand. 'Go back!' she whispered.

So he let the next wave refloat him then swam to rejoin the others under Magic Arch.

Fleur waded out of the water. The cove felt strange and different. The newly formed sand dunes stretched ahead of her in odd humps and hollows and the shallow roots of the fallen trees looked like gnarled witch's fingers reaching high into the air. A solitary cormorant had perched on the ship's weather-worn masthead, its dark plumage gleaming in the strong midday sun.

'Dad!' Fleur stopped to call through cupped hands. 'Mum! Is anyone there?'

The black bird took flight. It rose from the figurehead and flapped directly over Fleur's head.

'Dad!' she yelled again.

A muffled sound came from inside the hull.

Fleur's heart shuddered to a halt then thumped back into action.

From under Magic Arch Alfie and Mia heard Fleur call, saw her listen then set off at a frantic run towards the wreck.

'Come on!' Alfie said to Mia. They plunged from their dolphins' backs into the water then followed Fleur up the beach.

'Mum, Dad!' As she reached the wreck, Fleur made sense of the sounds coming from inside.

'Fleur – we're in here,' her dad's voice cried.

Realizing that Alfie and Mia were racing up the beach behind her, she scrambled up the curved hull until she reached the gaping hole where the palm tree had crashed through. She peered down into the hold. At first it was too dark to see inside. 'Dad, are you OK?' she cried out.

'I'm fine. But your mum is injured.' His voice was high and strained.

146

It took time for Fleur's eyes to grow used to the dark. 'Mum and Dad are down there,' she explained hurriedly to Mia and Alfie as they clambered up the hull. 'Mum's hurt.'

'Oh no!' Mia gave a small wail while Alfie positioned himself next to Fleur.

From inside the upturned hull James saw three heads silhouetted against the fierce sun. He sat with Katie's head cradled in his arms. 'I didn't dare to move her,' he explained.

'Mum, what's wrong?' Without any thought for her own safety, Mia squeezed past Alfie and Fleur, lowered herself through the hole then dropped three metres to the ground. She landed in soft, dry sand and was soon joined by the others.

'I'll be all right, Mi-mi.' Katie spoke with an effort through parched lips.

'She was knocked out during the storm,' James explained. 'We were desperate to find shelter inside the hull but the tree fell on her before we could make it to safety.'

Alfie crouched beside his mum and studied her

face. It looked pale and shadowy in the gloomy half-light and she had a deep cut on her forehead. 'Are you sure you're OK?'

Katie nodded weakly.

'How long was she unconscious?' Fleur whispered to her dad.

'For a few hours. Then it grew dark. There was no way I could leave her. But we didn't sleep a wink all night long, wondering how you three were doing.'

'We're fine,' Fleur assured him, but she knew it was best to get the bad news over with. 'But base camp isn't. There was a mudslide down the side of the mountain. It spilled over the cliff, landed on top of our shelter and smashed it to pieces. We had to sleep in George's Cave.'

'And we saw the dragon.' In the airless, cobwebby darkness Mia's voice sounded young and scared. 'It was hiding in the jungle. We had to run away.'

James reached out for her hand and held it tight. 'But here we all are – the Fisher family is back together again.'

'Safe and sound,' Katie murmured. Further explanations

would have to wait. She closed her eyes and heaved a deep sigh of relief.

They all held hands and sat for a while in silence, until a chorus of dolphins' whistles reached them above the sound of the breaking waves.

Straight away Mia jumped up. 'I forgot Stormy was here!'

'The dolphins brought us to Black Crab Cove,' Alfie explained. 'Dad, lift me up on to your shoulder so I can see out.'

James hoisted him up and, to his surprise, Alfie saw that the entire pod had swum to join Jazz, Pearl and Stormy in the foaming waters at the base of Magic Arch – around thirty of them: young and old, of different shapes and sizes, all shades of grey from almost white through metallic grey to dark charcoal, gliding under the arch then turning with quick flicks of their tails back towards the cove.

He recognized Marina, Pearl's mother, by her short nostrum and big bright eyes. She glided between the rocks ahead of several other full-grown adults then quietly circled the narrow bay. He lowered himself back to the ground. 'Mum, are you strong enough to hold on to Marina's dorsal fin and let her carry you back to base camp?' he asked with his fingers tightly crossed.

Katie opened her eyes and nodded. 'I took a bad knock on the head but yes – I'm sure I can do that.'

Mia and Fleur nodded eagerly. Fleur glanced up at the shattered hull above their heads. 'But we don't expect you to climb up there. We'll find a different way of getting you out.' She started to shove at the rotten timbers close to the ground and was soon helped by James and Alfie. Between them they pushed four long planks out of position. The planks landed in a sand dune that had silted up against the wreck. Once Alfie and Fleur had scooped the loose sand to one side, bright daylight entered through the new gap.

'Can you wriggle out through here?' Fleur asked her mum, who gritted her teeth and nodded.

'Slowly does it,' James cautioned as Mia, Fleur and Alfie went ahead.

Katie crawled towards the opening then paused and drew a deep breath to gather her energy. 'OK, here we go.'

Alfie showed Mia and Fleur his crossed fingers. Would their brave mum have the strength to make it out of the wreck, down the beach and into the water where the dolphins waited?

Katie inched her way through the gap, using her elbows to thrust herself forward. Emerging on to the dune, she was dazzled by the sunlight and felt sick and dizzy. But she was determined. Soon she'd crawled free of the wreck with James close behind her and Alfie and Fleur standing by to help her to her feet. Then they all supported her as she tottered towards the sea.

There, in the shallow water, Marina and two other adult dolphins circled slowly. Still dizzy, Katie saw their blurred outlines and took another deep breath.

'Are you sure you're able do this?' James asked anxiously. In the bright sunlight he saw that her forehead was not only gashed open but also badly bruised.

Katie nodded. 'How else are we going to get back to base camp? Wrecked by the mudslide or not – it's still the best place for us to hunker down and take stock.'

151

Alfie, Mia and Fleur waded ahead to meet Pearl, Stormy and Jazz. They caught hold of their dolphins' dorsal fins, vaulted up and sat astride.

'Dad, you have to lift Mum on to Marina's back,' Alfie told him. 'Then try getting up behind her and putting your arms around her waist and holding on to Marina's fin.'

'Will Marina be able to carry us both?' James wondered as he eased Katie into position.

'Let's find out,' Fleur said.

Pearl's mother rocked sideways as James hoisted himself out of the water. Katie slid and almost slipped back into the sea. But with James's arms around her she was able to sit upright, ready for the dolphins to leave the bay.

They swam slowly under Magic Arch, out into deep blue water – a pod of dolphins working together to help their human friends in need. There was no whistling or excited clicking, no leaping out of the water or show-off lob-tailing, no slapping of tail flukes or cresting the swelling waves. Instead they kept to the calmest waters, up along the coastline past Pirate Cave Beach and Turtle Beach until they rounded the headland into Base Camp Bay.

✳

As the midday sun reached its scorching height, James helped Katie to slide from Marina's back then led her to the shore.

Alfie leaned forward to pat the top of Pearl's head before plunging into the water. 'Thank you,' he murmured as she gave a soft, low whistle.

Mia hugged Stormy. Fleur said goodbye to Jazz. 'See you soon,' she whispered as the three young dolphins turned tail and followed the pod out to sea.

And then it was all hands on deck to help make Katie comfortable in George's Cave. They laid her down on the bed furthest from the entrance and used the yellow life vest from *Merlin* as a pillow. Fleur opened the first-aid kit and handed the packet of headache pills to her dad. Alfie fetched drinking water. Mia took off her yellow T-shirt, dipped it in the water and used it to cool her mum's hot cheeks. Once Katie had swallowed the painkillers, Fleur searched in the first-aid box and found the antiseptic

153

cream and a soft lint dressing for her mum's wound.

'Thank you ... good job ... thanks.' James went on tending to Katie. 'Get some rest,' he told her as he stroked her hair back from her forehead. 'Tomorrow we'll set about fixing a new shelter. Thanks, Alfie ... Good thinking, Fleury ... Thanks, Mi-mi.'

'Don't thank us,' Fleur reminded him as she stood at the entrance to the cave. 'It's Jazz, Stormy and Pearl that we all have to thank.'

'And Marina,' Alfie added.

Waves broke gently on the shore and the sky was pure blue after days of unbroken grey.

Something tickled Fleur's shoulder – a spider perhaps – so she absent-mindedly raised her hand to brush it away. But just in time she caught a flash of green out of the corner of her eye. 'George!'

Her gecko scampered from one shoulder to the other. He planted his tiny feet on her collarbone and

stared into her face.

'Hey!' Fleur's face broke into a wide grin. OK, so their mum had been injured, their shelter was wrecked and all their possessions had vanished under a river of brown mud. Plus, there was still the Komodo dragon to worry about. But lively, lovable George had survived the storm. Her little gecko friend was safe!

Chapter Twelve

As the sun passed its zenith and Katie slept soundly at last, Alfie and Fleur built a new fire outside the entrance to George's Cave.

They brought driftwood down from the wood store while James and Mia fetched dried grass and kindling. Then the kids gathered round as their dad directed the magnifying lens at the sun and used its scorching rays to set light to the heap of grass. They watched it spark bright red then heard the small crackle as it burst into life. Tiny yellow flames licked around the kindling which soon caught light. Wisps of blue smoke rose into the air.

'Stand well back,' James warned them.

The kindling set fire to larger pieces of wood. More sparks flew and the smoke thickened until at last they could relax, knowing they had fire once more.

And they had food for supper – chunks of dried coconut, fresh jackfruit and fillets of dried fish – as much as they could eat as they sat cross-legged around the flickering fire.

'I'm full,' Mia said with a happy sigh.

'Save some for your mum,' James reminded Alfie and Fleur, who were still chewing coconut. 'By the way, how come you brought that rusty old stuff down from the camp?' He gestured towards the coil of barbed wire outside the entrance to the cave.

'It's a barricade.' Alfie rolled his eyes towards Mia. 'We used it last night to keep out the dragon.'

'Ah!' James understood. 'Better safe than sorry – eh, Mi-mi?'

'It hissed at me.' She shuddered then crept closer to James. 'It really did! It had blood on its teeth.'

'Not nice,' he agreed as he gave her a hug then took her into the cave.

Alfie tapped Fleur's arm and led her away from the fire towards the headland. 'You know more about this Komodo than me. Is it really going to come and get us during the night?'

'Dunno. They hunt during the day mostly.'

'So we don't need to worry?'

She shrugged then shivered as a cool breeze swept in from the sea. 'Alfie, do you think we'll ever get back to how we were before the storm and the Komodo?'

'Maybe – if Mum gets better.'

'But will it be the same as before?' Would the happy, carefree days of exploring Dolphin Island, going fishing, rock-climbing and swimming ever return? Would Alfie make another map and would Fleur break off from her chores to study wildlife? Would Mia cartwheel up and down the paradise beach and skim stones at the water's edge?

Alfie didn't answer. Lost in his own thoughts, he gazed out beyond the reef.

'Alfie!' Fleur dug him with her elbow. 'Guess who's back!'

Jazz and Pearl rode the crest of a wave close to the reef. They plunged out of sight then resurfaced in a cloud of bubbles, tossing seaweed into the air and twisting and turning in the water as they caught it then tossed it again. Captured in the low rays of the sinking golden sun, Pearl surged towards the shore, spouting water from her blowhole, while Jazz performed his best tail-walking trick, clapping his flippers against his flanks before toppling forward into the foaming waves.

'Co-ool!' All dark thoughts vanished in the blink of an eye. Fleur clapped back at Jazz. 'What are you two doing here? Do you want to play?'

Alfie dashed into the water. He dived under and came face to face with a smiling Pearl, swam under her pearly pink belly then caught hold of her tail. She turned and dragged him out to sea. Jazz and Fleur sped up from behind. They rounded the reef in a whoosh of spray, then Fleur and Alfie broke away to watch Jazz and Pearl roll and twist in the water. They gave a loud whoop as the dolphins swam in rapid circles around them, clicking and chirping and churning up the surface.

Then, all of a sudden the games stopped. Pearl and Jazz came to a standstill and floated vertically in the water, their beaks in the air, flippers scudding close to the surface. Their heads were turned to the north, as if listening.

'What can you hear?' Alfie trod water and followed the direction of their gaze.

Pearl swam up and invited him on to her back. Jazz did likewise so Fleur sat astride, then they all set off up the coast, steering a straight course past the headland to Echo Cave Beach.

It was a wide bay with a smooth, empty beach edged by palm trees and backed by high cliffs – a place where the Fishers usually came to collect driftwood and any useful things that had been washed by the tide then dumped in the big cave close to the shore. Otherwise, Fleur and Alfie rarely visited the place and they had never explored beyond the far headland. Now though, Pearl and Jazz carried them right across the bay. They swam past the rocks marking the end of the beach then down a narrow channel into the next sheltered inlet where they slowed down and came to a halt. The low sun cast long shadows over the inhospitable, rocky shore.

Pearl gave Alfie her signature chirruping whistle then swam slowly into the bay. Jazz followed close behind until they came to a second inlet smaller and more sheltered than the first, where gentle waves lapped against the rocks ... and against the gleaming white hull of a sailing yacht.

At first Fleur and Alfie thought it was a mirage. It couldn't be a real boat – just a trick of the dying light.

'Do you see what I see?' Fleur asked. She let go of Jazz's fin to rub her eyes then looked a second time to see if she was imagining things.

Alfie stared without blinking at the glass fibre dream.

The sleek boat bobbed gently in the dark water. She was moored to a rock and her anchor was lowered – an offshore cruising yacht, over forty feet long, complete with furled mainsail with radar reflector on the mast, a polished wooden deck, lifebuoys and shining steel guard wires.

'It's not a dream, is it?' he muttered. 'It's real.' He read the boat's name printed along her prow: *Starlight.*

Then, before Fleur and Alfie had time to fully take it in, two men climbed the companionway and appeared on deck. One was tall, clean-shaven and suntanned, dressed in a green T-shirt and white shorts. The other was older and stouter, with grey hair and wearing a blue polo shirt and matching shorts and deck shoes. They stood hands on hips, staring at Alfie and Fleur sitting astride their dolphins.

No words were spoken. Alfie took in more astonishing details – the dark blue canvas sprayhood that covered *Starlight*'s cabin, her TV antennae, boarding ladder and blue style lines that ran the length of her gleaming hull. Fleur held tight to Jazz's fin, still unable to believe what she saw.

The man in the green T-shirt leaned over the starboard guard wire. 'Hey there – does either of you speak English?'

The older man beckoned for them to come nearer.

A boat! An actual boat! Alfie held his breath. After eight weeks and three days of hoping for rescue then losing all hope, after fifty-nine days of marking the calendar stick and battling to survive, *Starlight* glistened white and perfect as she bobbed in the dark water. On board she would carry all the equipment needed to navigate the hazardous Torres Strait – an electric compass and sophisticated network systems, a chart table and touch-screen plotter.

Fleur saw the tall stranger's mouth move and gradually made sense of his first words – 'Does either of you speak English?'

'Yes!' she called back. 'We're from England. Our boat sank.'

'Fifty-nine days ago. No one came to rescue us.' Alfie's voice croaked as he tried to explain.

'Just you two kids?' The younger man glanced at the one in the blue polo shirt in open disbelief.

'No. We're with our little sister and our mum and dad.' Fleur took a deep, stuttering breath then turned to Alfie. Her eyes were wide, her hair blown back from her tanned, freckled face. 'A boat, Alfie – it's real!'

The older man spoke to his companion then beckoned them again. 'OK, kids – climb aboard. We had a problem with our bilge pump during yesterday's storm so we were forced to find safe harbour. It was touch and go for a bit. But we made it, and earlier today Sam here managed to fix the electrical fault. Don't worry – we'll soon have you out of here.'

With a sharp intake of breath, Alfie leaned forward

to stroke Pearl's domed head. 'Did you hear that?'

She answered with a series of rapid clicks then tilted sideways to allow him to slide gently into the water.

'Oh, Jazz – I have to go,' Fleur sighed. Tears came into her eyes as she watched Alfie swim towards the boat then climb the ladder. 'We're going to have to leave Dolphin Island.'

He clicked quietly then carried her slowly towards the boat.

The two yachtsmen in their crisp, clean clothes waited for her to join them.

Jazz let her wrap her arms around him for the very last time. He felt warm and soft. There was a kind look in his beautiful dark eyes.

The water lapped at his flanks as, still crying, Fleur slipped from his back.

'Here – let me help you.' The older man knelt on the deck, leaned forward and offered her his hand. 'You and your family will be off the island and heading back to civilization before you know it. Where can we find the rest of your family?'

'We'll show you the way.'

Fleur climbed the ladder and stood beside Alfie on the smooth, shining deck. They looked down at Pearl and Jazz, swimming in circles and whistling gently as they prepared to leave the inlet.

'Welcome aboard. I'm Laurence.'

His low, growly voice and short grey hair reminded her of Granddad Tony. He had a kind, wrinkled face.

'It's pretty amazing that the dolphins let you ride on their backs,' Sam commented as he started *Starlight*'s motor then pressed a button on the cabin control panel to raise her anchor. The diesel engine roared into life and the propeller began to turn. 'I've seen that sort of thing in a dolphin sanctuary but never in the wild before.'

'Pearl and Jazz *are* amazing.' Alfie watched their dolphins swim side by side between the headlands into clear water, lit by the fiery ball of the setting sun. Their sleek bodies undulated through the water with scarcely a ripple – graceful as always as they halted fifty metres out to sea.

'What are they waiting for?' Laurence took up

position at the prow of the boat as Sam steered her expertly between the rocks.

'To show you the way to base camp,' Fleur explained with a faint smile at Alfie.

He shrugged and smiled back. *Naturally – what else?*

Chapter Thirteen

Mia stood alone on the shoreline of Base Camp Bay. It wasn't fair – she'd been in George's Cave with her mum and dad when Fleur and Alfie had gone off without telling her. Now she had no one to play with as the sun went down.

She stooped to pick up a flat pebble then skimmed it across the smooth water and counted the bounces: three – four – five then *plop*. It disappeared below the surface, creating rings in the water that widened then faded. She considered drawing a hopscotch grid in the wet sand, decided against it, then practised walking on her hands instead. She took seven – eight – nine steps before her arms gave way and she landed in a heap next to the coil of barbed wire and the conch.

Cool! She seized the shell and took it to the water's

edge then gave an experimental blow. Out came a low, wet squeaking sound. She tried again. This time the squeak was louder – almost a proper note. Once more and this time she had a major success. A long, high note rang out across the bay. Moments later, Stormy swam into view.

With a little squeal of delight, Mia ran into the sea to meet her dolphin playmate. He swam around the reef and leaped in a clean arc out of the water. Then he put

in a sudden spurt of speed and was with her before she was waist-deep. He whistled loudly then nudged her and smacked his tail flukes against the surface. *Come on, Mi-mi – hitch a ride!*

With one joyous bound she was on his back and hanging on to his fin as he turned and sped away from the shore. As he took her down below the surface, he blew a cloud of bubbles and swam with her amongst the wafting sea grass until they reached the coral reef

and the darting angelfish and glinting silversides. Then up for air with a whoosh and a gasp. Mia clung on to Stormy's fin and laughed out loud as they headed north towards Echo Cave Beach.

'Hey!' she cried when she spied Pearl and Jazz rounding the far headland and swimming towards them. She blew them loud kisses 'This is so much fun!'

Alfie and Fleur's dolphins cruised towards her, spouting water from their blowholes and blowing raspberries. They breached the water and sent spray showering down over Mia's head and shoulders. She closed her eyes tight shut and when she opened them again she saw a big white boat sail around the headland.

A big white boat with two masts, like *Merlin*. She heard the smooth throb of its engine and saw three figures standing at the prow – a man and two kids. Her heart skipped and jumped as she recognized them. 'Hey, Alfie! Hey, Fleur!' She waved both arms high in the air.

'That's Mia,' Fleur told Laurence in a matter-of-fact voice.

The seasoned old yachtsman took in the sight of a small, tousle-haired kid in a yellow T-shirt being carried across the sparkling blue ocean by a half-grown, dark grey dolphin. 'Now I've seen everything,' he murmured in disbelief.

Fleur and Alfie waved back at her. 'Look what Pearl and Jazz found!' Alfie pointed over his shoulder to the streamlined boat.

Sam switched the steering on to autopilot and came out of the cabin for a closer look.

'So that's your kid sister,' he said to Alfie. 'How old?'

'Seven.' Seven years and eighteen days to be exact.

Laurence gave a nod of admiration 'She's at home in the water – I'll say that for her.'

As Pearl and Jazz met Stormy then took up position to either side, Mia stood up and balanced behind Stormy's dorsal fin. She spread her arms wide like a surfer as the three dolphins swam playfully across the bow wave made by the speeding boat. She laughed as Stormy crested the wave then carried her wide of *Starlight*. Still giggling, she lowered herself to sit astride his back.

'Stop showing off – let's go and tell Mum and Dad the good news!' Fleur cried.

So the dolphins swam in a wide curve then headed south into Base Camp Bay where James stood at the edge of the beach with his arm around Katie's waist. The sun was sinking behind the mountain and all they could see at first were the outlines of three dolphins rounding the headland.

'Mum, Dad – Jazz and Pearl found a boat!' Mia yelled. 'Really and truly – it's following us.'

James and Katie stood in stunned silence as *Starlight* hove into view. It was everyone's dream rolled into one. Katie clutched James's hand.

'You're not seeing things,' he murmured as *Starlight* steered a steady course towards the beach. 'It's not the knock on the head that did this to you – it really is happening.'

*

Sam dropped anchor by the reef as Laurence inflated the life-raft then rowed for the shore. He shook hands with James and Katie and introduced himself – Laurence Middleton from Southampton, sailing the

Strait with his son, Sam. Quickly he explained what had brought them to Dolphin Island – the high winds that blew them off course, the storm damage to their bilge pump, the safe harbour beyond Echo Cave Beach.

'Those are three amazing, exceptional kids you have there.' He jerked his thumb towards Mia, Fleur and Alfie who were saying goodbye to their dolphins in the shallow waters.

'Kids, come quickly,' James called. 'I need you to help me break camp.'

While Katie agreed to be rowed back to the boat so that her cut could be properly cleaned and bandaged, he waited for them to join him before springing into action. 'Our first job is to make sure we put the fire completely out,' he told Alfie. 'Fleur and Mia, scout around to see if there's anything you want to bring with you.

Alfie kicked sand over the flames and watched them die. He kicked more sand on top of the pile to make sure. Then he followed the girls up the beach.

They stood together at the edge of the mudslide,

surveying their poor crushed shelter and the mess of fallen trees and noticing a family of monkeys perched motionless on what had once been the roof. The macaques stared at them from under their fluffy crests, twitching their pale moustaches and swishing their tails.

'Relax – we're giving you your island back,' Fleur said with a hint of sadness. 'I don't want to take anything with me,' she told Alfie and Mia quietly. 'I'd rather remember how things were before the storm.' Blue moon butterflies and red admirals, cockatoos and cassowaries and of course macaques – she would hold them all in her memory.

'Me neither.' Mia put her hand over the mother-of-pearl charm hanging around her neck. She had Monkey and this dolphin necklace that Alfie had given her for her birthday – that was enough.

But Alfie picked his way through the dried mud. There was one thing he would take if he could find it.

'What are you looking for?' Mia trod in his footsteps.

Without answering he stepped up on to the smashed platform and cleared away a mess of palm fronds and

174

sections of flimsy wall. 'We left it by the door – it must be here somewhere. Yes!'

'The calendar stick!' Mia cried.

Alfie grinned and held up the long, notched stick. 'Here's my souvenir!'

*

At the last minute, Fleur changed her mind. She picked up the conch that Mia had left lying at the water's edge and handed it to her dad who carried it into the life-raft. In the dying rays of the evening sun, Laurence rowed him and a few of their possessions out to *Starlight*.

'Don't be long,' their rescuer warned Mia, Alfie and Fleur. 'The tide waits for no man.'

The kids stayed to make their last footprints in the wet sand. Fleur slipped into the cave to say a quiet goodbye to George. 'I lifted the lid off the food store,' she told him. 'There's plenty of coconut and jackfruit in there. Don't let the monkeys eat it all.'

He squatted on his ledge, glowing bright green in the dim light. He opened his wide mouth and flicked out his tongue.

'Yeah – goodbye, George.' She sighed then walked

out of his cave to see a large, pale full moon sail clear of the horizon. The first faint stars began to twinkle in the violet sky.

Mia skimmed one last pebble. Alfie waded into the water ahead of Fleur and Mia to say the hardest goodbye of all.

Pearl, Jazz and Stormy waited for them close to the shore. Together the dolphins and kids formed a circle. Alfie reached out his hand to touch Pearl. She turned her head to nudge his shoulder. Mia gave Stormy a gentle stroke. Fleur leaned her cheek against Jazz's side. Not a word was spoken as they swam on towards *Starlight* then climbed the ladder on to the deck.

The engine purred, the propeller turned and she glided out past the reef. Fleur stood between Alfie and Mia on the bathing platform at the rear of the boat. The evening breeze was cool against their cheeks as they watched their dolphins swim quietly in their wake. All was calm. The island grew smaller and they felt the rise and fall of the boat as she sailed on through the waves.

Then Pearl, Jazz and Stormy broke away to give the

Fisher family one last display. They breached the waves in unison then criss-crossed through the water straight ahead, broke away again and rolled belly-up, squeaking and whistling as they flapped their flippers against their sides.

'There goes Jazz!' Fleur smiled at her dolphin's high-low whistle before he dipped under the boat then down into the depths.

Stormy leaped clear of the water and called out to Mia. He plunged deep under the surface then up again with a spray from his blowhole and a final shrill whistle.

'Bye, Pearl!' Alfie locked his gaze on to gentle Pearl as she surged ahead of the boat.

She smacked her tail flukes on the water then dived down out of sight.

Close to the horizon, their pod waited. The dolphins would come together and roam the seas, play their games under Magic Arch and in the mangrove swamps. They would feed and rest, swim on through the deep clear water of the Torres Strait, but for years to come Pearl, Stormy and Jazz would always return to the white, untouched shores of Dolphin Island.

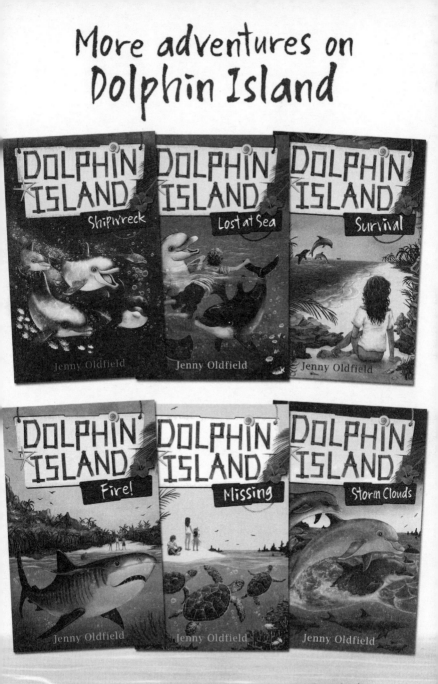

Jenny Oldfield

Born and brought up in Harrogate, Yorkshire, Jenny wrote
stories and made tiny books complete with illustrations even
as a child. She went on to study English at Birmingham
University and then worked as a teacher, before deciding to
concentrate on writing. Jenny writes novels for both
children and adults and, when she can escape from her desk,
likes to spend time outdoors in the countryside walking,
playing tennis, riding and travelling
with her two daughters.